Jack's Diary

MARCUS DAVIS

STEPS Publishing

STEPS, LLC STRATEGIC TRAINING, EMPOWERMENT PROGRAMMING & SOLUTIONS

Jack's Diary

Edited by: Dr. Catherine Williams and Janaye Jordan
Book Cover Designed by Janaye Jordan

Printed by STEPS Publishing

First published by STEPS Publishing, October 2016
ISBN: 978-0-9962011-9-3

About STEPS Publishing
STEPS Publishing (www.stepspublishing.com) is an emerging leader in helping to develop the talent and skills of individuals desiring to write and publish their materials. Our mission is to support the goals and dreams of writers by providing such products and services as: biographies, novels, training manuals, short stories and plays.

The STEPS Publishing methodology is an eclectic one which helps authors weave their dreams, experience and passions into reality- their books.

For my parents, Velva and George

May 9, 1887

As I look in the steam covered mirror…I see many faces. I see a young boy with short, black hair, a pale face, and no smile. I see a confused teenager full of rage. Then I see me as the man— no, the demon-- that I have become.

I smile at the deed that I have just committed. I wipe blood from the fresh scar under my left eye. Her final mockery of my face. She deserved it; they both did. The investigators may say this was grisly and the person or monster that did this went too far. But, this is no crime. No; I consider it payment, or maybe even artwork. You see, I loved her. I loved Sarah. I smelled her auburn hair, sweat, and perfumes. I loved the way she laughed, sang and danced around the house when I was there. I loved to watch her. I even watched as the man on top of her pleased her better than I ever had a chance to.

My hands…my horrible hands are covered in crimson. There are still bits of flesh under my nails. But who cares- no one *ever* cared about me. No one ever really *saw* me. This is what makes this artwork. This will always be my masterpiece. No one will know my name or face. Clean. I need to clean this whore's blood off me. I am beginning to hate its putrid, rusty smell. My clothing is saturated with bits of hair. I need to draw a bath. I need to relight the furnace. I'll walk from the washroom past my pieces of art and head downstairs to the wood burning furnace. This bath will make me feel better, will help me rest my tired muscles.

"Cleanliness is next to Godliness," is what my dead mother would say. I chuckle as I strike the match.

There's a noise upstairs... the match burns my fingers, but I don't feel it. I listen...

A voice in my head- it's my mother. "They're still alive." They can't be. I feel the match burning my fingertips black.

THUD!

There was no mistaking the sound this time. I needed to go look to be sure. I dropped the match and headed upstairs as fast as my legs could go.

My mother told me, "They are going to the police. You are done for!"

"Shut up!" I yelled aloud in a cracked, winded voice.

I made it to the top of the stairs in what felt like an hour. I do not remember when I grabbed the butcher's knife from the chopping block, but I knew I needed it. I reached for the doorknob, grasping it tightly. It was surprisingly cool in my blood-soaked hand. I could hear my heart beating in my ears. The scar under my eye was burning from the sweat. I opened the door and feverishly scanned the room. The man was up, shuffling and staggering around. The moon gave me plenty of light to do what needed to be done. I paused for a moment, remembering Sarah's voice as she called his name while reaching her third climax, "Ohh, Edgar!" How often had he paid her for her "services?" Did he know how angelic her voice was when she sang while bathing? The feelings from earlier came back in a blood boiling rush. I knew I had plenty of time for this one. This one would not be as sloppy as earlier. It was a little difficult killing both of them together, but I could see that I was not as efficient with good ole Edgar. I was only able to get one of his eyes and partially slit his throat the first time. This time I would complete this painting.

I ran towards him, burying the knife in his shoulder. I began yelling what I heard my mother saying in my head, "YOU STUPID, STUPID BOY!!" with each hack of the knife. He may have screamed if he could. As I withdrew the weapon, I saw bits of bone and cartilage fly through the air.

I began to shriek with laughter as this six-foot-five man's life drained from his good eye. My mother is silent.

August 17, 1887

Months have gone by. I ended up moving deeper into London, and I've begun working as an assistant mortician. My name here is Thomas. It's been easier than I thought to continue on with life after murdering my first love. The men I work with always ask me to have a few at the tavern. I always decline, but tonight I will be there. But, no doubt, them will be there. Them- who spread diseases to hard-working men. Them- who open their legs for small amounts of coin.

I always enjoy when I have to cut open a woman. I'm starting to feel as though I should do this forever. I was thinking about it at work tonight.

"They are disgusting," I whispered, mimicking my mother's voice.

"What's that?" Jim, the head mortician, was helping me move bodies to different rooms.

"Oh nothing," I quickly replied, snapping back into the now. "Hey, wanna down a few after we clean up?"

His face brightened. "I was beginning to think you had a distaste for the lot of us. Sure, my wife is off with her boyfriend tonight," he chuckled. I smiled. Jim had no clue of my plans.

"Well, tell her if she can handle two, then why not three?" I laughed, grabbing my crotch.

"You are one sick bastard, Thomas!! C'mon, let's finish these bodies up, mate." Jim laughed. I think that he would have turned out to be like me if he did not have a sense of humor. I guess losing a son to a horse and carriage accident will do that to you.

We finished up and headed to the tavern. Jim and I sat at the bar with two others: Wexler and a black man named Tobias. At work, Jim and I handle the cutting and stuffing of the bodies. This is where I learned all I could about human anatomy. Wexler and Tobias handle the embalming and make-up, respectively. To this day, I don't know why Jim hangs with those low lives.

Upon our arrival to the bar, Wexler started in with as many racist jokes as he could to piss Tobias off. Always talking about niggers and Jews. The tavern was everything I imagined it would be. The harlots and jezebels were on laps and allowing men to grope and poke in all sorts of places. The more I watched, the sicker I became. After my third drink, I felt the strong urge to vomit. Jim patted me on the shoulder.

"Hey there friend, how're ya?" he asked. I could almost taste the alcohol spewing from his pores. His words were slurred and I barely understood him.

"Fine, mate. Just enjoying the view," I said with a grin.

"These dumb whores aren't worth the coin you'd spend on them," he said. Thinking the same thing, all I could do was laugh. I downed the rest of my drink and headed to the lavatory. The bathroom was nothing to write home about. It was dark, dank and cold. No real light except for four lanterns that burned. There were two at the doorway and two at the back of the room. I washed my face in the rusty basin, looked in the mirror, and almost screamed. There was Sarah, both eyes missing, maggots spilling from her mouth. I smelled the mildew of dying flesh and decayed clothing. She gripped my shoulder and I could feel her bony, icy fingers. As she spun me around, I let out a small yelp. She had on a black evening gown.

She then whispered in my ear in a crackly, raspy voice "I need *friends*. Give me *friends*."

I fell before her, bumping my head on the sink. I looked up at the skin hanging from her skull and all I could do was nod. She looked toward the door as Wexler walked in, unzipping his pants.

"What's on ya, mate?" He smiled a toothy grin. I looked back for Sarah- she was no longer there.

"Tied on a few too many," I said, standing to my feet. I ran my fingers through my tangled, matted hair.

The mirror has become my new enemy. Sarah informed me tonight that my time as an artist is not done.

Leaving the tavern, I was the soberest among us. Tobias and Wexler stumbled off to their respective homes while Jim and I walked on.

"Thanks for hanging wit' the lot o' us, mate," he slurred. Thanks came out *thanksh*.

"Ah, don't mention it, mate." I overdramatized my drunkenness.

After dropping Jim off at his door, I went in the opposite direction of my home. I headed back towards the tavern. Under my shirt, carefully tucked into my pants, was an icepick that I kept for protection. However, Sarah provided me with another use for it tonight. Someone needed *'friends.'*

I walked up the cobblestone street as if I were patrolling. I felt too noticeable. I decided to find a place to hide. There was a large underway where the moonlight did not shine and no street lamp could penetrate the darkness. I do not remember when the voice in my head changed from my mother's to Sarah's, but I knew I wouldn't be hearing the last of it.

"Excellent, my love. They will not see you coming at all." Her voice was very dry and raspy. She sounded as though she had not drunken anything in days.

"Thank you dear," I whispered. The sound of my own voice made me jump. I clutched the ice pick closely to my chest. My breathing felt loud and labored, but I think it was just the echo.

Hours passed and still nothing. I had carefully slid the ice pick back in my pants, past my belt hook, when the rain began to fall. I began to step away from my hidden area and I heard something familiar. I instantly went back to my place and listened intently. It was a woman's laughter, and as soon as it registered, my heart leapt. I pulled the ice pick back out of my belt loop, trying to hear her over my steady breathing. There was a woman and a young man walking hand in hand. I already could tell by her dress that she was a whore. A *lady of the night* is what they like to be called. With her breasts almost exposed, she coerced the young, well-dressed man she was with into an alley. In my haste, I bumped into a trashcan and dropped a bottle, making a loud, crashing noise.

She must have had excellent hearing. The alley was at least ten paces away and she still turned and asked in a scruffy, uneducated voice, "Who's there?" *There* came out *thea.* She took a few steps forward and I almost shrieked as a cat jumped from the trash behind me with a loud, meowing noise. I felt as though Sarah had been looking out for me in the cold night. The harlot plodded off, laughing in the alley. I heard her echoing down the dark walkway. I quickly skipped across the cobblestone street and stopped at the mouth of the walkway, slowly peering around the corner and hoping that the least of my head would be showing.

The alley was a dark and dirty place between two tall buildings. There were trashcans and old bits of clothing on the ground, long since molded. The stench was almost overwhelming, but that wouldn't stop her from doing what she wanted to do. I caught her getting on her knees and taking the young man's member into her mouth. How disgusting she was. I wanted to look away but was unable to. My mind was racing because there were so many questions. Should I kill them both? No, it wasn't his fault. These hussies spray a certain chemical in the air and make it so the males cannot even deny them. Therefore, I would wait. I waited and waited. He finished and she swallowed. I waited as he lifted his pants and paid her her 'well-earned' coin.

I don't know if I tasted my own sweat or the disgusting rainwater from the top of the building, but I licked my lips all the same. I waited patiently for the man to leave the scene. My heart was beating violently in my chest as I creeped behind this stain on the human world. I closed in on her and I knew she felt my presence- too late- as I grabbed her around her mouth. I flashed the ice pick across her face to feel her breathing increase. I made sure that I buried it in her throat first to make any screams she may have had turn into gurgles. I noticed that with every stab, the urge to masturbate came strong. I tried to make it happen as fast as I could, but she was not losing enough blood. The arm that I used to hold her was getting tired. I lost count after thirty-six strokes. She finally fell to the ground and I with her.

My breath wasn't catching as fast as I wished it would. So I sat and I waited. Eventually, I heard movement from the other side of the alley. I was instantly on my feet. My mind and heart were racing. I looked up the alley in the direction of the slow, shuffling noise that was closing in on my temporary domain, and I saw the beam of a flashlight slicing into the darkness with tendrils of sight. I got as close to the edge of the alley as I could and crouched down. Sweat began making puddles in my clothing. I automatically assumed it was the police. They usually travel in pairs, so I would do what I could with at least one of them. I saw the beam of the light shrinking as it was getting closer to its originator. Then a voice.

"Helloooo...anybody there? If there is any funny stuff going on, I will call the police and take care of you post haste. I live upstairs and I am not afraid to defend what I own."

The relief washed over me and I almost let out a sigh. Then for good measure he said,

"I do own a pistol."

The man nearly jumped as the cat swished past his light beam making a loud hissing noise. I may be losing my mind, but the cat did look at me as it walked past. It must have been Sarah.

"Goddamned alley cats!" The man almost shrieked as the beam spinned away while he turned away from what he thought it was he may have happened upon. I waited what felt like ten minutes before I stood again. I walked over to the recently killed plague and noticed that her eyes seemed to be following me. Please let this be the friend that Sarah wanted. But she did say friends with an 's'. So this may not be the end. I don't know if I can handle this anymore.

I began to walk home. I was smiling for some reason. I couldn't help myself. I ran up the stairs to my room in the dilapidated home that I rent out. As soon as I got inside, I leaned against my door and I reached in my pants and had at it. Right there at my door. I then made it to my bathroom and vomited in the tub.

What type of creature am I?? What am I becoming? I should seek help, but I *hate* Them. They have to pay for their transgressions and nastiness. I'm lying on the floor in my bathroom and looking at the ceiling. I cannot continue to do this, Sarah. I will not. I won't.

"We have only begun my love." The words are clear but floating away in my room as I drift to darkness.

August 18, 1887

A knock at the door awakened me today. It was more of a thudding, and when I first awoke, I was thinking that I was back at Sarah's and there was someone alive who shouldn't be upstairs. I jumped up slightly, bumping my head on the tub.

The knocking turned into banging.

"Mr. Wilschire, this is the Scotland Yard Constable. Please open up!"

I didn't know what to do at that moment. All I could do was freeze.

Again, the same deep, loud voice, "Mr. Wilschire, if you are home, please open up. If not, we will have the landlord allow us to enter. This is your final warning."

I scrambled to my feet and took a quick peek in my mirror. I looked haggard. I quickly ran some water on my face and turned the hot water on in the bathtub.

"I'll be right there!" I shouted aloud while running to the door.

The blinding light from outside informed me that I was well into the afternoon by this time. There were two bobbies dressed in official constable uniforms. The first was a tall, heavyset man with a deep, dark mustache, and the second was cleaner cut with blond hair. He looked to be in training. The third person, bringing up the rear, was the stupid landlord.

"Yes, that's him. He is a straaannngggeee one," said the old landlord with his white furry eyebrows. "He is the weird one I was talking about."

I tried not to grit my teeth as he spoke about me directly in my sight.

"Can I help you bobbies?" I said, clearing my throat. I surprise myself on a daily basis. I had nothing but a large amount of rage building up inside me because I couldn't rip the old man's eyebrows off and shove them down his throat.

The first to speak was the heavyset constable.

"Good day, Mr. Wilschire. Is it Thomas Wilschire?"

I nodded.

"Yes, well we were told that you used to live on Commercial Road, and we would like to ask—"

"You need to answer these fine gentlemen's questions," interjected the landlord, or really slumlord, as Sarah and I like to call him.

"Mr. Vanschlatt, your services are no longer needed. Thank you," stated the older constable sternly.

"O-oh, of course. Please let me know if you need me. I am downstairs, sec—"

"Second door on the right; we understand," finished the younger constable.

"I don't know about that one. That one is a straaannnggee one," Mr. Vanschlatt commented once more and shuffled down the stairs to his room. The officers watched as he walked off and then turned their attention back to me. Had I not looked back at them shortly before they looked back at me they would have seen the disdain on my face. Just to be sure, I reopened the conversation.

"Can I help you, fine gentlemen? And please do come in. I apologize for the mess; I wasn't expecting company," I charmingly added with a smile. I offered them both a seat, and as the younger officer began to sit, the older heavyset one loudly cleared his throat in objection. The officer in training snapped back up from his half-seated position.

"Yes, what can I help you with, Constable?" I asked.

"Well, firstly, my name is Constable Blacksmith and this is Constable Ratcliff, and we just have a couple of questions to ask about Commercial Lane if you don't mind- since you used to live there."

I tasted the slight flavor of metal in the back of my throat and my heart began to slowly trot in my chest.

"Yes I did; go on." I swallowed.

"Well, yes, there was a visceral double murder that occurred on that street, and we would like to know if you knew a Sarah Timmelton."

I needed to think quickly. I spoke as slowly as I could so my words didn't tremble.

"Please excuse me, gentlemen, I was just drawing a bath," I said very smoothly.

I rushed to the bathroom with sweat beginning to form on the back of my neck, palms and armpits. What could I say? "Yes I knew her, and I cleaved her and her stud to tiny pieces?"

I squatted down, placing my chin on the tub, staring into my reflection in the water and thinking of my next move. I was slowly feeling the walls closing in. As I slid my hand into the steamy water, five icy fingers grabbed my wrist. *Sarah!*

"Noo," she whispered in that same crackly voice. "We have only begun."

As she spoke those words, I snatched my hand away, clinging to my wrist. The bony hand seeped back into the water as if it was homogeneous with it. I stood and peered into the empty bathtub. I knew now what needed to be done. I headed back down the corridor with a newfound confidence.

It's as if Sarah is giving me energy, as though she *wants* me to go on and kill as many people as I can.

I returned to the two constables and my voice almost frightened me as it escaped my lips. "Sorry again, gentlemen. You said Sarah Timmelton, Constable Blacksmith? That name does ring a bell." I smiled again. Then I waited. "No need to jump the gun now, dear boy, you need to make them eat from your hand," I thought.

There was a quick glance between both officers and Blacksmith spoke with mild concern, "Everything alright, Mr. Wilschire?"

In an effort to maintain my act, I furrowed my brow.

"Of course Constable, why do you ask?"

The two officers stole another quick glance at each other as if to make sure they were seeing the same thing, and then the younger spoke.

"Well, you look as though you've seen a ghost, Mr. Wilschire."

I felt a large cackle growing in my chest and quickly responded to stifle the laughter.

"Oh, no, no, no. I scalded myself on the hot water trying to turn it off. But back to our initial conversation about Sarah....?"

"Timmelton," Blacksmith responded.

"Oh yes! I did hear of her. She lived a few doors up from me, if I remember." It was going smoother than I could ever imagine. I did not want to sound as though I was stalling, so I continued. "And using my memory as a reference, she had a heavy flow of male callers."

"So we have been informed," Constable Blacksmith stated.

"What we are wondering, Mr. Wilschire, is whether there is any other information you can give us. Were there any arguments or was any one of her gentlemen callers more aggressive than the others?" he continued.

I gritted my teeth on this question, for all I could remember was watching good ole Edgar and his large phallus entering her. Paining and pleasuring her at the same time. I snapped back.

"No Sir. Not at all, Constable. I am sorry to not be of better service to you. I mainly stay to myself, as you can see," I stated, glancing around my apartment.

Taking out his notepad from his front pocket, Constable Blacksmith wrote something on a sheet, teared it off and handed it to me.

"This is my number. Should you remember anything, please call. If I am out, please leave a message with the operator."

"Will do." I smiled quickly and walked them to the door. I gave them some time to leave and then walked to the window. As I stood there, the younger of the two constables glanced twice at the window, as though he had not seen me standing there the first time, with a confused look on his face. I waved as they finally walked down the road. I looked at my wrist as my wave slowly trailed off and there were four finger-like burn marks there. It looked as though someone with a hand of fire grabbed my wrist. I fell back on the floor, cackling madly.

Sarah's getting hungry and I need to feed her. And feed her I will.

August 30, 1887

I've been making sure to lay low over the past few weeks, and every once and a while I have a run in with Sarah. I quit my job to become a garbage man. Jim was very upset to see me go. He told me that I was a natural the way that I made my cuts on the cadavers. I don't know why I took this new job. Something was telling me to get it, and I am so glad I did. Yesterday, we were clearing out an alley near the police station and I came across a gold mine. There were old files that had been discarded for space purposes. It seems as though they were supposed to be destroyed, but it looks as though someone was not on his job. But, back to the reason why they are a goldmine. These files contain all the solved crimes from at least five years ago.

This is an extreme find. I sorted through and found at the very least twelve to twenty solved murder cases. I almost shrieked with glee as I flipped through the old files. Since working this job, I have learned more and more about the area that I am in. I have learned so many streets and found all sorts of alleyways. Finding this pile of old paperwork in the trash will make my artwork easier to pull off. People only see the trash, but it takes a true genius to see the treasure.

I am starting to have the ability to tell when Sarah is in my presence. The air begins to get thicker and it becomes very cold. As I reached into the 'trash' and flipped through some of the files, the cold air became unmistakably heavy. She began her crackling whisper in my ears. I felt the slightest freezing touch on my shoulders through my clothing.

"Take the murders. Learn all you can, my sweet." She crackled her request from decayed lips. Now, I continue to go through the files that I stuffed in my overalls. I know these will come in handy.

Later on, I began my studies. I took notes and even left my home to get a blackboard and chalk to have something to erase in case of evidence. It's funny, because I always feel as though I will be caught. However, no longer will I have these fears. Sarah laughs. I am beginning to wonder why she is so focused on me murdering these women.

After several hours of studying, I drifted off into a deep slumber. I awoke with a beauty grinding her hips on my shaft. I could not see her face since her hair was covering it. I reached towards her and cupped her breast, and she revealed her face. To my surprise, it was Sarah. She gave me this innocent, schoolgirl smile and continued her up and down rhythm on me. As I stared at her face in awe, a small black crack formed on her left cheek. Her blue eyes broke from mine in shame. She covered her face and began to sob. I reached up, pulled her hands from her face, and noticed that the crack had grown. A small spider crawled from the crack and skittered into her mouth. At that moment, she jumped off me and ran away.

By then, I had gained focus of my surroundings. I was in a large black forest. I felt something slithering on my hand, flinched, and sat up. I was on a bed of black moss and vermin. The thing I felt on me was a large, black snake. I jumped of this slimy 'bed', and I could now hear whispers of other women. I raised my trousers and began walking towards Sarah's sobs. The trees in this coal-colored forest did not match each other. There were dogwoods next to weeping willows and different fruit trees with rotting fruits. For some reason it was becoming more and more difficult to take regular steps. I looked down and saw thick, black weeds and fallen tree branches clinging to my trousers. With each step I took, there were squelching sounds. Looking down, the ground was no longer just black moss, but it was becoming a thick, tar-like substance.

I looked back up to see a large balboa tree in the distance. I heard her cries from there. The tree was in the middle of a large, dark and cloudy field. I had to make it to that area. I struggled for what seemed like days before I reached the base of the tree. The tree had an uncountable number of vines all over. Sarah was at the top. I could hear her. As I reached for the closest vine to climb out of this now waist deep goo, one of the fallen branches reached from the tar, grabbed my arm and stopped me.

Then, the voices of the women were clear- here and there. '*STOP!*' and '*NO!*' could be heard. I trudged further still. I *needed* to get to the top of the tree. The branches that were hindering me had become female hands. Every time one of them touched me, I heard a voice whisper as clear as a bell. It was as if they superseded Sarah's sobbing the moment they touched me.

"Free us!" was one of the last ones that I heard.

I heard a small, bubbling noise below in front of me. I looked down and there was something coming up from the bottom of the oily substance. The pale face of my last victim emerged and stared at me. For some reason, this made me want to vomit. Every time she opened her mouth to speak, black beetles, maggots, and more of the oily substance crawled from her lips. Her skin was sunken in and her eye sockets were deep grey circles in her skull, but I could still make out her features. And the smell—oh, to the holy heavens, the smell was almost murder in its own right. Being that I am a garbage man, I instantly recognized the rotted meat smell, but there were other smells intermixed. Like ink and fermented milk fragrances coming from her mouth. Combined, it almost brought tears to my eyes.

"You..." she began. I can only assume that the beetles and scum were choking her words from her voice box.

"…Cannot…" I leaned forward as much as I could to try and hear her. The other hands were keeping me from making much forward movement.

She continued, "…keep this…"

The woman's face looked up in the direction of the top of the tree. I glanced up and saw nothing but darkness and black leaves. I looked back down at the face in the tar ocean and she was back to staring at me, but this time there was fear in her eyes and she no longer spoke. I watched in horror as her face began to bubble like the black fluid did earlier. I was trying to look away, but for some reason I could not. This thing—this abomination's face, was melting away. The skin was hanging from the muscles of her face like some type of melted skin cheese. Moments later, there were only muscles, tendons, and eyes left on this skull thing in front of me.

I then heard hissing close by and instantly thought of the large snake, but when I looked up –there she was- Sarah. Her hair was now black and her skin was a slimy, sticky gray. She was upside down on the tree, so her hair covered her face again. Her hands had lost some of the skin on the fingertips, so now she had bony claws that dug into the oily, black bark. She lifted her head to look at me. I still heard her sobs and hisses as I looked into her coal black, shiny eyes. She wasn't crying normal tears, but black, oily fluid ran from her eyes. Her chest and stomach were firmly on the tree as though she was giving it a death hug.

I was frozen by her transformation. Fear crept up the back of my neck. There are no words that I can form to put myself at ease. She shifted her gaze from me to the skull thing. The hissing became more dominant over the sobbing. Her hand reached out in blurring speed towards the skull. Had I blinked or sneezed, I would have missed it. Sarah palmed the top of the skull thing, and the whole time it was looking at me. Sarah then began a twisting, wrenching motion like she was opening a pickle jar. I was trying to close my eyes, but it did not matter, for the crunching, snapping noise of the vertebrae in her neck was almost enough to make me faint. The branches that were holding me back were now holding me up because I surely would have fainted by then. I wanted to scream for her to stop. The skull thing still did not take its eyes off me.

I watched as Sarah snapped the thing from its root like a potato from the ground. Sarah finally jumped from the tree and stood on its roots. I don't even know if that was to keep her from sinking into the tar like I was or if she planned it that way. She squatted down to admire the head of this skull thing. Well, at least that's what I thought she was doing, until she pulled the thing to her face and a long greenish purple tongue extended from her mouth and licked the top of the skull thing's head. But for some reason, the skull thing never took its *fucking* eyes off me.

Sarah then opened the jaws of the skull thing, sucked its tongue out, and began chewing it like gum. She went to the eyes and sucked each god forsaken one from its socket. When she chewed, the eyes burst in her mouth like a tiny balloon filled with water or a juicy jellybean. She then sucked the rest of the eye tendril, and it slapped against her lips like spaghetti. I had no choice but to watch her finish eating the entire skull. She then walked toward me but stayed on the root. She picked me up like a baby and held me there. Her breath was hot and filmy with indescribable smells.

"*You took this from me,*" she crackled.

Her mouth then elongated and she let out a scream that sounded like every animal I have ever heard in one. But, I realized it was actually me screaming, and I was back in my bed fighting the sheets. My sheets were so wet I assumed that I had urinated on myself, but found out it was sweat. For some reason, my sides were itching and burning. I reached for the mirror and lifted my shirt to reveal scrapes and cuts all over my ribcage as though I had walked through a thorny thicket.

My voice has gone horse due to screaming throughout the dream. I still feel as though I haven't slept. I am missing something. I don't understand what I am supposed to get from that dream.

September 20, 1887

Every day that I am not working, I am busy with my projects. I've begun getting deep into my studies early in the mornings, just like mama taught me. I feel that the murderers who have been apprehended seem to have no wits about them. One man was caught by his hair color, which was based on a witness description. So, I shaved my entire body. I also did non-extreme things, like buying gloves, which was easy. But, other things that seemed simple, like buying the right shoes, were very difficult. I cannot wear my exact shoe size, because one woman was caught by a shoe print. To combat such a trivial method of being caught, I have all sorts of different shoe sizes. Some are slightly larger or immensely smaller. I went out and also bought a few different trench coats.

Now, this is where the process becomes tedious. For each killing, I do not want to use the same weapon. For each coat, I took the time to stitch little hidden pockets that I can tuck different knives and small scythes in. It's easy for law enforcement to find a person based on the weapon they use. Or even still, the areas that a person murders in. Luckily, as a garbage man, I know the Scotland Yard area very well. It took me three weeks, but I obtained all the proper utensils for my artwork to be just the way I want it. I can tell Sarah is pleased because she has been quiet for these past few weeks. This night will be the first time I go out with the new information I have. I will be sure to put it to good use.

It wasn't as dark as I would have liked for it to be. I was dressed in a long black trench coat and a nice top hat. My clothes seemed to give off the appearance that I had money to spare. That was the exact look I was going for. About five women approached me while I stood under the street lamp. Neither Sarah nor I liked any of the women for some reason or another. I was on the corner where the Whitechapel church is currently under construction. I needed to leave this area because too many had already seen me. Being that I was in East London, I knew there were at least two taverns close by. The walk should not have been too far.

As I walked down the main road, I saw all types of whores taking johns and many men enjoying their wares. It disgusted me. It made me think of the times my mother made me study arithmetic.

Her name was Andrea –my mother, if you're wondering. See, no matter what you think of me, you are with me. You need to know what I come from. My mother was the best teacher of my life.

"Look at you," she would say, standing in front of me smelling like alcohol, cigarettes and a random man's sweat.

"You look and smell like shit, you little shit," she would laugh to me.

At seven years old, I didn't understand why I was treated this way. I was beat on a daily basis. After finishing with one of the many men she let penetrate her, after my father was gone, she would have at me. I remember at one point she seemed to have a fetish for tying my hands to the top of a

25

wooden chair and beating my knuckles until they were bloody with a
leather strap.

You are nothing but a burden to me," I heard from her over and over.

I would be locked in my room for days with nothing but water while I
would hear her play with the many men she 'knew as friends'.

I walked into the tavern and sat at the bar. The scene is always the same, women on laps and loud men trying to get under their dresses. The bartender walked over and asked me what I wanted.

I cleared my throat, "I'll take a whiskey and ale," I said.

About two hours and four ales later, I headed back out. The ales help keep Sarah quiet in my head. I also see her less and the targets more. As I walked further up these cobblestone streets, many of the women were in groups or with johns already. I had an idea of what I was looking for. She needed to be small and very innocent looking. There was a commotion at another tavern a few streets up from me. A woman of the night was involved and was getting thrown out. She was wearing a lacey undergarment with a brownish white dress. She was perfect. Sarah would be pleased and I could tell. She had a pure face and not one wrinkle in sight.

"Fuck ya all to shit, then!" she yelled at the building, flipping the bird.

I walked faster, viewing her from across the street. Ten feet up from her, there were two men smoking. They were all drunk, of course. I found the closest alley and waited for her to pass them. Her heels click-clacked against the pavement as they began to proposition her.

"I got sumfin' fa' ya ta suck on roit 'ere," one of the neanderthals said, grabbing his crotch.

"Ya 'aven't enough coin ta make me kiss ya, let alone suck on ya tiny lil' willy," she laughed.

I walked past them on the opposite side of the street. I then made my way in front of them. I walked ahead to see where the darkest area was. I reached into my pocket for a handkerchief and a small bottle of chloroform – another find on one of my trash hunts—and slowed my strides. I heard her and the two men continue to exchange words and I waited. Her cheap heels began their momentum again towards me. Luckily, the street bended, so the men wouldn't be able to see her soon.

All of a sudden, her heels stopped their click-clacking. I was so caught up in my own thoughts that I hadn't realized they stopped, and for how long I didn't know. I continued to walk forward. I was too afraid to look back. Then I heard,

"Oi, why doncha move along there guv'na?" She spoke in a slurred, drunken tone.

I could feel the sweat forming on my gloved palms. I quickly re-pocketed the chloroform and kerchief and turned around. In an effort to make sure that every word was understandable, I cleared my throat.

"Pardon me, madam." I almost did not recognize my own voice leaving me.

"Hmm... A gent'le man me eyes 'ave landed upon. Ya not like these ova' tossers at are out and about I see," she responded.

This was all I needed, a small amount of dialogue. Looking at her then, I saw why I no longer heard the click-clacking of her heels. She was

27

holding them in her hand. She seemed as though she was trying to seduce me, holding her shoes over her shoulder like a purse.

"'Atta moiee foine hat ya got there," she said, rubbing the brim of my top hat.

I did not know what to say. I am not in the practice of even breathing the same air as them. I felt the nausea rising and didn't know if it was the ale or her smell. I almost flinched away from her but was able to keep my composure.

"Yes, well I am a fancy man with fancy tastes, my dear," I said with a toothy grin.

"Well if ya got tha roit coin, then ya won't get any fancier than this 'ere prime ass!" She exclaimed, patting herself on the rear. *Is this how these transactions go with men besides me?* I wondered as she grabbed my hand.

"I know the perfect spot luv." She smiled, leading me further down the street toward the harbor.

I didn't know if I was comfortable in such an open area. The docks had a large circular area with huge stone tie-offs for different boats and ships. But, my issue was with the back end of the curve where there were houses and bungalows. There were plenty windows for a peeping tom to look out of. The purpose of this murder was to see if I was able to abscond with this. The funny thing is I knew I only had one chance to get this right. I don't mind being a gambling man.

She let go of my hand and did a drunken spin to look at me. She leaned against one of the large stone pillars while I stood in front of her.

"So wot can a lil' wench loik me do ta make ya noit bett'a?" she playfully asked.

I reached in my coat pocket and jiggled what coins I had.

"Would I be less of a gentleman if I asked for a sample first?" the voice I am using stated.

She smiled and grabbed my crotch to feel my girth.

"Well, well, I see sumbo'ee's red'ee. I don't moind givin' ya willy a lil' sample," she said, getting on her knees.

She unzipped my pants and took my already hard penis into her mouth and did what she was good for. I pretended to moan as if in ecstasy. She reached her hands up to my chest, blocking my coat shut. It was now impossible for me to reach in and get what I needed. So I grabbed both of her wrists with my left hand and slid them far enough over so that I may reach into my coat. With my right hand, I went into my lapel, slowly slid out my ice pick, and raised it over my right shoulder.

"Filthy whore!" I grunted, thrusting the ice pick towards her head.

When she heard me, she was beginning to look up and tried to flinch away, but it was too late. I was aiming for the top of her head, but upon her quick movement I buried it into her left temple. There was a muffled balloon popping noise and her left eye rolled into the back of her skull. Whatever was sliced through, it broke like a dam, and blood splashed from her nose all over the shaft of my penis and bottom of my stomach. I could not stifle my laughter as I continued my pick as deep into her skull as I could. She tried to push away whilst her eye rolled around like a marble. As I grabbed her head and pushed my member deeper into her throat, I saw blood bubbling from her left eye socket and run down her cheek. When she fell back, streams of blood flew back into her hair and began to pool around her head. I could not stop laughing until I began coughing. I looked into the puddle and saw the face of a lunatic. My eyes were the size of eggs. Sweat fell from my face and I labored to breathe. In the process of stabbing her, I dropped my hat. My shaved head had red droplets on top. This made me snicker a little more. I turned back toward her body and pulled my sharpest butcher knife out. Then the real fun began.

I cannot say that my childhood was the greatest. But, I made do with what I had. After the death of my mother at ten, I was shipped to the lovely Happy Sunshine Orphanage. What a funny name, since there were no happy times or sunshine there. There were monsters, goblins, and ghouls there. We had a lovely headmistress named Ms. Applegum. She was a mean bitch who always carried a ruler with her that was made from the strongest wood known to man.

Most times, a small rap on the hand makes a child listen, but Ms. Applegum would always go steps further. If a child crossed her radar, that ruler would get its maximum usage. At the age of ten, she was the largest woman I had ever seen. Her hair always seemed wet and fell down her cheeks in gray, yarn-like strands. She had three or four hairy moles on her upper lip and to this day, she is the reason I will never find moles to be beauty marks. She was a fat, sloppy and downright disgusting excuse for an orphanage director.

Don't get me wrong, it wasn't just her abrasive looks, but her fucked up behavior. For instance, churches, for God's sake, would donate used clothing and food to her sick justification of a place for children. She would smile her brownish, gray-toothed smile and say things like, 'Thank you,' and, 'You are too kind.' But when that door closed, she would turn with a nasty sneer.

Anything she received that she did not sell herself she would give to her second in command, her disgusting and just as fat little snot of a son, Jeremiah Applegum. This little shit was short and fat but strong. Whenever he worked, the children would pray for death. He would give whatever Ms. Applegum gave him to HIS children or bait the children in with whatever toys or food he received and get them to enter his quarters. Whatever happened to them was something I knew nothing about at first. He was such an ass that he would wait until dinner, torment a random child by smacking his face into their plate of food, and not even give them anymore. I hated them both, but Ms. Applegum was the one in charge and ran the whole hellhole.

At one point, I dunno when, but Jeremiah began having a strange fetish for little boys. Now, I knew about sex thanks to my mother, but I never knew about men wanting other men, or boys for that matter. But I promise you, Jeremiah taught me painfully well. All this was under the close tutelage of Ms. Applegum.

I looked around after I got my wits about myself. I saw no one, so I began making my cuts. I had taken the time to sharpen my blades very well, so when I began to slice into her still warm breast I had no resistance. I only removed my gloves so that I could physically feel the parts that I would take with me. It took me only moments to cut her left breast, nose, and liver from her. I don't know why I took these parts, but I think that Sarah really wanted them. It was a shame that she only moaned once when I began to cut her. I can only assume that the life had all but left her at that moment. Or, that may have been all she could have done with the blood loss. At any rate, I finished my cuts and began to leave with my parting gifts. The alcohol that I drank was beginning to fade and Sarah was seeping back in. I had just begun to walk away when she grasped my shoulders.

"*She has something of ours.*" Her words whispered so close to my ear that I felt as though they were freezing.

I stopped midstride. I was close to leaving the harbor and I thought, *what could she possibly have of ours? I mean, of mine?* I almost chuckled- what did I mean 'of ours?' But, back to my thinking, I felt the top hat on my head; I had all of my blades and my gloves. I thought harder and I didn't remember if I had ejaculated down her throat or not. I didn't want anything to be traced back to me by any means. *Just in case, I must resolve this*, I thought. I looked around again and walked back to her body. I once again removed my butcher's knife and began making hacks at her already exposed chest cavity.

Now, I don't know if it seems as though my travels as a garbage man would make me better at my artwork, but it has. As time was becoming my enemy, I hacked as hard as I could at her sternum and the ribs around it. After what seemed like hours, her bones finally gave in with a satisfying *snapping* sound.

With her upper innards exposed, I reached into the cooling warmth of her chest and found the esophagus. It became much more difficult to pull out then I originally assumed. After trying, I cut the tendons attached to her tongue, which snapped like pulled rubber bands, and finally pulled it free. Just for safe measure, I took her stomach. Time was beginning to flee fast and the day was creeping over the horizon like a sunlit tablecloth. I had to make it home before it got too early. As I left the scene, I threw the pieces of my craftwork into trash barrels on the routes that I had in the next few hours. The further away I got, the calmer I became. I finally made it to the back alley of my domicile and climbed the fire escape. I made sure to leave my window unlocked so that I could make a clean entrance.

After getting in, I still had plenty of work to do. I took the time to clean every utensil –even the unused ones—and placed them where they belong. My top hat, trench coat, gloves, pants and undergarments, I bleached. Now, the issue was getting the items down to the incinerator in the nude. I did not want to put any clean clothes on without taking a bleach bath. I opened my door and snuck my head out to take a look. I didn't know what time everyone wakes. I only had two flights to go down, so I was sure that I could take care of this fast. The incinerator is very simple to manually operate, so I slipped out. I can only assume it was close to five o'clock.

I made it to the broiler room and tossed the items in and watched them burn to make sure that there was nothing left. This took about thirty minutes. I ran back up the stairs and peeked around the corner of the hallway. No one; but as soon as I got to my door I heard another door open. I made it in, did my regular routine of masturbating and vomiting, took a hot bleach bath, and slept for two hours.

September 21, 1887

They always say that a criminal returns to the scene of a crime, but in my case, I had no choice. I began my route earlier than normal. All the barrels with the parts in them had to be collected, because every Monday the collected trash from the previous week was burned by noon.

As I got closer to where my previous artwork was, I saw a large crowd of people gathered as though they were watching a game. Many constables were there for crowd control. Looking around, I saw Constable Ratcliff. We had not made eye contact and I needed to make a decision. I didn't know- if I spoke with him, would I be an assumed criminal for returning, or would he just realize that I was working there? I thought that I needed him to see me. I felt that if I was seen now, there would not be any suspicion of me possibly being the one who did this. I decided to go with the working class, nosey-Nancy character. I felt Sarah's cold, wet fingers caressing the back of my neck.

"Constable Ratcliff!" I called out, dumping the last trash barrel with any possible evidence.

The main dumping barrel is basically just a cart with a horse attached in the front and a large container in the rear. I walked around to the front and fed the horse a carrot. When I looked back up, I saw that Ratcliff had not heard me.

"Constable Ratcliff!" I shouted again.

His concentration broke from the group and peeled through them. He took five or six steps towards me and by the time he got to me, I was in full character.

"Seems as though you have someone famous in your little area, huh?" I asked.

"Oh, no—Mister Willcott?" he asked.

"Wilschire." I smiled.

"Yes, Wilschire. No, there was a murder," he said.

Since I was in full character, I covered my mouth, took a deep breath, and raised my eyebrows.

"My word, Constable!" I exclaimed.

"Yes sir. By the way, what size shoe do you wear?" he curiously asked, looking down at my feet.

"Ni-nine and a half, I believe, I haven't purchased shoes in a while," I stuttered out.

He pulled out his notepad and flipped a few pages. "Hmm…too small," he mumbled. "Well, Mr. Wilschire, I don't have any more questions. Please be careful at night bec—"

At that moment Constable Blacksmith appeared through the crowd of people.

"Oi' bloody hell, Ratcliff. You're supposed to be on bloody crowd control aren't ya?" he said exhaustedly.

"Y-yes sir, but Mister Wil—" he began.

"I needed to ask if I could get past, Constable Blacksmith. I distracted him, and I apologize," I finished, winking at Ratcliff.

He made a small nod towards me. I don't know when I became the normal conversationalist, but it is working for me.

"Wait, who are you again?" Blacksmith asked.

"Wilschire, Sir," I said.

"Wilschire? Thomas? You look somewhat different," he said, questionably scratching his head under his cap.

The uniform that I wear comes with a cap, which I removed, exposing my bald head.

"Yep, with this job, the long hair kept the smell of trash far too long after washing it," I quickly made up.

"Don't let the Chief Inspector see you over here talking to some random person," Blacksmith said quietly.

I quickly chimed in, "No, Constable. I just needed that trash barrel over by that wall and I'll be on my way."

Blacksmith took a deep breath as if to calm himself down. I knew there was no way that I could see my artwork again. I just needed Blacksmith to think I was a complete moron.

He calmly stated, "Mr. Wilschire, unfortunately this is a crime scene and I am sure your supervisor will understand your reasoning for not getting this barrel. Now, if anything happens to you behind this one barrel, I will personally write him a letter."

"You just made my workload one barrel easier. You gentlemen have a wonderful day," I said, lifting my hat once again and walking off.

The further away I got, the angrier I became. Retracing our conversation, he said it was a crime scene. No! No! No! It's art, IT'S ART!! How can they not see what we saw? The beauty is in the criminal details. I finished my normal route with my horse in tow. I went into our work shack where the master keys were located. I unlocked the fence that's used to protect people from the burning trash. After carefully pitch-forking the trash and my art pieces on the previously smoking embers, I realized I was late. I didn't mind; I can comfortably listen to my boss go on about this later. This *had* to be done. While watching the fires burn the body parts and smelling the burning flesh, I could remember things…

December 14, 1865

Miss Applegum would always knacker about pretending—and I use that word loosely—to teach us proper schooling. She would really only use this to make good use of her primary weapon, that infernal ruler. I remember little Richard Brittle was asleep at his desk when she sharked around close to him and Thwack! Crunch! See, Richard got the name Brittle because he had a rare disease that made his bones very easily broken. This disease coincidentally made him sleepy as well. She had hit him with the straight edge of the ruler and broken his middle and ring finger.

Anyway, this place was no place I could learn anything about but pain and how to be angrier. You would think that, at the least, the nursing facilities would be up to par, but the nurse there would always turn the other cheek. For some reason, she would let little, fat Jeremiah get all the feels on her robust, tender body. Speaking of Jeremiah and his feelings, when I became twelve years of age, he showed me what men who didn't like women acted like around boys. This sickening act was what ultimately sealed everyone's doom in that orphanage.

September 21, 1887

I was so enthralled by the flickering flames that I began to lose track of time. I got up from my crouched position, turned to lock the fence, and standing there watching me was Constable Blacksmith! I was so focused on the fire and my memories that I had not realized he was there. I also didn't know how long he had been standing there.

"Sorry to bugger about there; you dropped your work gloves," Blacksmith stated. "Hey, don't you all usually have someone ta burn the trash?" he asked with a raised brow.

"Ah, yes, Constable. I thank you. They always seem to slip from my back pocket," I said as sheepishly as I could.

When I reached for the gloves, I continued, "My supervisor tells me I am going to need my own budget for these gl--" he then snapped his wrist back as if to say 'Ah-Ah.' I knew he was waiting for me to answer his question.

"Oh, and yes, I like to pursue my work to the end. Some of the men who do the burning will leave the work for us. But we end up in trouble for getting the barrels here late," I quickly made up.

"Righto, good mate, but to sift through it like you do?" he hypothetically asked, handing me the gloves. He walked past me towards the fire. My already quickly beating heart went even faster. He stood over the fire with his knuckles on his hips. What was he doing?? I walked over to him with my pitchfork under my chin. I began tensing my shoulder and arm muscles, waiting for the moment that I would strike for his neck or stomach. His body would need to go into the fire immediately.

"These two murders have to be related somehow," he mumbled.

I instantly relaxed my muscles and acted as though I did not hear him.

"We have to be close to finding this bastard," he continued.

I saw he was now deep in his thoughts. My day was done and I needed to plan my next move. I do at least now know that I may be scot-free with the murders. I looked at the remaining embers and wanted to laugh out loud.

"Constable, I am sorry again that I cannot be of any assistance to you. Ratcliff told me there was a murder back there. Was it bad?" I asked, concerned.

"Yes, Ratcliff has an issue with keeping things to himself. But yes, there was a murder and it was pretty bad. And we are standing here with our willies in our hands," he replied.

"Well, if it's any consolation, when you first came to my home I knew you would be determined to find this monster," I said to him, not breaking my eyes from the fire. He thought that I was distracted by the fire, but Sarah was there giving me the words to say to him. She was staring from the fire at me- that's why I couldn't feel her there as usual.

"Well, thank you for the vote of confidence, Mr. Wilschire," he stated, turning away from the burning trash. "But that and half pence will get me a haircut."

As Blacksmith walked off, I continued to watch the embers as Sarah burned away with laughs that only I could hear, well after I locked the fence and left the trash yard.

September 25, 1887

I needed to figure out a different method of attack. These two murders that I have escaped do not necessarily mean that I'm guaranteed to keep up my luck. I had to go somewhere else to continue feeding Sarah. I was too close to home to be practicing. So, I've decided to go outside of Scotland Yard. I was able to find a little shack-like cottage that I can use as a hideout. Due to the recent drop in the economy, people will have to move into or away from the city. These places that are left have not been looked at by anyone sometimes, and people are able to live in them without anyone knowing. This gives me a place to actually begin my notes and stash my 'paintbrushes'. This hideout is also perfect because of its basement. I can be completely uninterrupted here, and I can always come back when I have learned more.

It took me a while to make sure no one lives here. I would come out at all different times of the day and night. I didn't know if this was a good idea or not, but what about this was? My sanity has lost any chance of questioning. I don't even know if I am getting proper sleep. This cottage is only about ten miles out west of Scotland Yard. I've been able to find at least a few women out and about. This will keep Sarah sedated for very short spells.

I don't know if a certain type of woman I murder keeps her longer than others. Like for instance, I stalked a woman who was just looking for a place to stay from the rain. She came in expecting no one here, but still said a mild "hello" before she came in. I was in the middle of sharpening my tools, and as soon as I heard the creaky noises of the steps outside, I quieted everything and blew all the candles out. It amazes me how many women talk to themselves when they are alone. This one, I did not mind her screams so much for it was a stormy night and no one was on the road the night that she was out. I assumed that she would be a whore when I began. A very simple kill this would be. I already had an idea of quick ways to kill, so this would feed the wrath of Sarah. She seems to get hungrier the further away I stay from the London area. This time I used my chloroform. I have grown pretty talented with the use of my chemicals through the years.

November 10, 1865

My mother's was the killing that really started me on my path. I don't know when I made the final decision to end her career as my vile warden. I think it was the final time she used me as an ashtray for her cigarettes. I was ten years old when I'd finally had enough. She would do all sorts of nasty things to me, then ask me to fix her dinner, where she would eat in front of the fireplace that my father left her to warm her evil heart. But, allow me to go back. My mother only became this evil after my father was out of the picture. Before that, she used to sing me to sleep when I was afraid and caress my hair while I was dreaming. She and I were almost inseparable.

But, for some unforeseen reason, she changed when we arrived to London. We used to live in America, but my father was originally from London and wanted to move back there. I was three at the time that we arrived in 1858. Times had become hard when we moved here. My mother instantly realized that she could make her own money by offering her body to random men. Of course, my father didn't agree, or care, if I remember, but I do remember that he either left or died from alcohol. Either way, at four, my mother began to abuse me. She came to hate me. I learned early that I needed to not stress this, for it would pass. But, one night, I was fed up. I had not eaten that day and she came home with the biggest steak and large potatoes for herself. I would not allow her to comfortably enjoy it.

I was told to cook, and I waited until she was good and drunk before I served her. She was never quiet. She would scream at me to hurry before the next man came. I was tired of hearing his and her moans every few hours. She would claim that she was doing this for me. My mother had blonde hair and a beautiful face with barely any fat on her body. This is what made her so easy to be used by these men.

So anyway, I wanted to see that beauty fade. I began cooking her steak on the stove as well done as she normally liked it, as a good little boy should. I boiled the potatoes in a nice large pot over the fire. I remember it as though it was yesterday. I was so afraid to reach under the sink for the rat poisoning when she went to the lavatory. I heard her in there freshening up and washing the last man's semen from her body. I poured the poison in the boiling water for her to enjoy with her potatoes. I put away the box and began to mash the side dish. Every once and a while, I would scoop a small spoonful to smell the food- just to see if the potatoes smelled any different. I arranged her meal perfectly. I brought it to her and sat the warm plate on her lap. As soon as my hands were off the plate, in a quick, drunken, and accurate swing, she slapped me to the floor. My mother had practiced the backhand so well that even with my ever-growing height, she was able to floor me all the time and laugh.

"Took you long enough, you turtle," she spouted.

I laid on the floor with tears in my eyes but a smile on my face as she started on the steak and potatoes.

"There are lumps in the potatoes!" she yelled, with bits of food flying from her drunken mouth.

I still watched. She only stopped once to burp. I was nervous for a few moments, but she cleaned the rest of her plate with the speed of a hungry, feral dog. She threw the plate at me, went into the bath, and cleaned herself up. A knock at the door startled me into getting the plate and cleaning the dishes. I expected to see her fall out and die as she returned from the bathing room.

"Hold your horses!" she called out. "Carry your ass to bed now and ignore whatever you hear," she growled at me.

I scurried off and waited until I heard her door close with them on the other side. I wanted to know what was taking the poison so long. I crept back out of my room, next to hers, and crawled to the key hole to get a good look. There was a medium built black man with a bald head in the room and he started undressing. He was from London and you could tell he didn't do too well in school.

"Oi' ya sick ah sumfin?" he asked my slimy mother.

"No, why do you ask?" she questioned.

"Ya swea'en loik an ole pig on slaughterin' day," he said.

"I like the way you use your words," she said, reaching for his shoulders to kiss him.

Andrea was sweating, and it took me a while to realize it myself. Her now naked body was almost dripping, like she had run all day and had just come to a rest. I began to sweat as well, but for a different reason. Mine was from anticipation of the upcoming event. He climbed on top of her like a dog and began his thrusting, and she began her moaning. Her moans were beginning to sound more painful. I didn't know if he was hurting her, or if the poison was doing what I assumed it would have done earlier. He turned her over, placed himself in between her legs, and started

43

thrusting very hard. She then howled and pushed him off, but there was no time. She spewed vomit all over his face and it splat all over her place in the bed. He rolled off her and spat out what had gone into his mouth.

"Fokin shite!!" he yelled.

Andrea could not gain any control of her facilities at that moment and she urinated and soiled the entire bed. She then convulsed for what seemed like an eternity before finally stopping. I covered my mouth and tried not to laugh. He grabbed his clothes and I ran from the door but fell as he raced out. I was very clumsy at ten. He stopped for a moment and only gave me a quick glance before he dashed from the house.

I peeked around the corner and called out quietly, "Mom?" in the quiet room. My voice seemed very loud.

Her left hand was clenched while the right hand twitched a little. Her eyes followed me around the room. It smelled like urine, feces, and recently swallowed food. Vomit stuck to her cheek and began to dry in clumps in her hair. Now, I know that when a person is poisoned, they can still see but may be paralyzed. She grunted, watching me approach her bed. The prison that her life was in was granted a pardon and was departing from its bodily cell.

"…Nnng…little…shit…," she strained to tell me.

There were two more solid grunts as she clawed at me. Then, for some reason, I instantly did not want this anymore. I grabbed her hand, fell to my knees, and began to wail. At ten years old, watching my first victim fall prey, I did not think this all the way through. I needed her as she had needed me. I mean, sure, she was no proper example of positivity as a mother, but she still was all I had left at that time. But now, there was no one. I did not realize how important it was for me to stay with her and her with me. *Moreover, to make it all worse, the black man who reported it was hanged for the crime. I mean, now I can laugh at the loss of anyone's life thanks to her, but at ten, I cried myself hoarse. By the time the two investigators came, I said nothing. One constable actually slapped me to try to get some information out of me. I was considered a mute for the next two years. I was then taken to Happy Sunshine Orphanage where I painfully found my vocal chords.*

September 30, 1887

It is difficult to get many kills like Sarah and I want. I have noticed something very particular about Sarah. She seems to be more interested in killings that are known by many people. I cannot just kill without anyone knowing about it. Like, the second or third woman, I pounded her head in with a rusty spade. I had to actually chase her through the woods before I was able to fling a stick and trip her. And boy, did I work her pretty face over. Then, using the sharp spade end, I decapitated her and removed her hands and feet. So far, that one gave me the best erection. When I finally finished burying the body, I looked up and Sarah just stared at me and turned away.

"What...? What? I am doing the best that I can, my love," I said to the empty night, falling to my knees and out of breath.

Apparently, I have to perform my killings back in the city. She won't be satisfied until then. I committed three more on the trip back. The first, an axe to the head, another, a slit throat, and the last was a scythe across the abdomen. That one was actually quite fun. I had caught her coming around the bend, grabbed her from behind, and sliced her open. I threw the scythe to the ground and like in my mortician days began ripping her intestines out, and did I laugh. I laughed so hard that she got away and began to grab for the innards she was losing, but then tripped over them in the process. This makes me howl. Now, before I am judged, these were whores. I am sure of it. All they do is ruin homes and body parts. I have seen men die behind their dirty snatches. So what if I have tears of laughter in my eyes when I walk over and slice the upper portion of her head off?

I am able to continue back and forth on my days off to my little, comfortable cabin in the woods. However, deep into London is where Sarah and mine's relationship really flourishes.

October 13, 1887

Just stalking whores for their demise does nothing to keep Sarah sedated. She has an incredible thirst. At the very least, we are back in London. To her, I am only working, and not really working, if you catch my drift. Another odd thing that I am seeing with her is that she seems to have more skin, or flesh, when I do more killings.

I've been on a new route since coming back to work after my leave of absence. While on this route, there's been a woman sitting on her stoop. I haven't really paid her much attention, but for some reason I cannot take my eyes off of her face. She is nothing amazing to really look at. She has long, silvery black hair and freckles all over her skin. But, it is her face that I cannot remove from my mind. She has a large scar on the left side of her face, which covers her eye. Her right eye is a normal green color. There are other scars of course, but that one does something to her eye. It makes it discolored like a hazy, cloudy grey.

Now, many people walk past and laugh, or throw her some coin as she sits on her stoop. But, she isn't rude about it nor does she give the money back or curse back at the ill-refuted people. She may have become accustomed to it or she just doesn't care what they say or think. All I would do is wave and give her a nonchalant smile. I never approached her.

One day, Sarah showed up and it made me pause. I did not know if I wanted to kill her or not. The longer that this goes on, the more I am learning about Sarah and I. And, this is only a sidebar, but we must both be on the same accord when it comes to considering the art piece. I was unhappy with adding this one to my gallery. Again, Sarah turned away from me.

"Take a pickter, why dontcha? It'll last longer," the scar faced woman asked.

I am learning to respond quickly. I snapped back into reality.

"I—I apologize madam, I just noticed that you seem to be in need of assistance with the cleaning of your windows," I lied.

She leaned back and looked at me, surprised. I knew then that she was interested. She stood up, exposing her seductive frame. She then looked up at her windows, covering her bad eye. At this point, I was confused. *Can she see out of the eye?* Looking at her backside made me instantly erect.

"Seems like ya got an offer fa me," she replied, turning back to me.

I couldn't kill her. In this putrid town, I am surprised there are other women with intelligence. At least, her dialect isn't as broken as some of these other harlots here. I only obtained my ability to write, read and even speak properly from two people who are dead now. Sarah appeared behind her and began shaking her head negatively. I ignored it.

"Yes, well I am inclined to help when I have free time," I replied, walking to the front of my horse.

She said as seductively as possible, "Well, I may be inclined to use your services. Wot's ya name, kind sir?"

"Thomas Wilschire, Madam," I quickly replied.

She knew I was attracted just by the way she licked her teeth and smiled. She stepped off her stoop to approach my horse and me, rubbing his mane. I could only see her hand on his mane and her waist by the nose of him.

"So, Thomas, what about him, hmm? Wot's 'is name?" she asked, crouching under the neck of the horse and invading my personal space.

I do not wish to sound like some sideshow gypsy or something, but it seemed as though her eye was looking past my physical form and directly into my spiritual. I know that sounds crazy, but it is true. Then again, what about my life so far sounds normal, or better still, not crazy? When she reached up to touch my face, I flinched.

"Aww…you poor thing. I can see yer scared. Wot or who hurt you?" she asked, clutching the hand she was soon to touch me with.

How did she know there was pain? I instantly became angry. I had to end this impertinent banter.

"Madam, I apologize, but I have to finish with these barrels," I said, coldly reaching around her to grab my coworker's stirrups. She touched my wrist as I went past her.

"Tabitha," she stated quickly.

"What?" I questioned.

"My name is Tabitha," she said.

"Yes, well Tabitha, is it? Some people have to work for a living. I do not have to time to waste on nonsense," I said impolitely.

"Well, Well, Mr. Wilschire, yer in serious distraught aren't cha? Well, ya know where I live. Whenever you are ready ta assist me with those windows, let me know," she said confidently, pointing to her home.

I could only nod. I made up my mind. She will die. Sarah laughs. How did she know about my pain? She will know pain soon.

October 16, 1887

Over the past few days, I have avoided her road or peeked to see if she was there before collecting on that road. This killing will be for Sarah. I will find a nice spot to take care of her and that blasted eye to make Sarah happy. I've begun my research again. This time, I went into the sewage tunnels. I stayed in the murky, wet, and downright stinky under-city trash ways for hours with a notepad and pocket watch. I would go on opposite days of the week. For instance, the first week it was Monday, Wednesday, Friday, and Sunday. The following week I researched the other days. I pretty much had what I needed, but I gave it one more week for safe measure. After these three weeks, I drew up a plan of attack. The only thing I now needed was to see how to get into her home. Of course, the back alley would be the best way in.

That following day as I collected trash, after realizing that she wasn't there, I sneaked into her back alley by climbing the fence. Upon landing, I was almost taken aback by what I saw. There was a large, beautiful garden. Flowers and vegetables were all over the place. Almost everywhere I turned, there was something wonderful to be viewed. She had different large figurines all over. This was so unexpected. Her back door was slightly opened. I ran to the nearest statue and hid.

Waiting for a few minutes, I heard humming coming from inside the house. She came out with a basket and began to pick her tomatoes, potatoes and turnips with care. She spoke to each one she picked it, saying things like, "Aren't you a beaut," and, "Nice job, Tabitha." I watched intently from behind the angel statue as she finished and stood, heading back to her door. Suddenly, she stopped, turning to her bad eye side. I laughed in my head, thinking that she shows this eye when she wants to intimidate someone. Unfortunately for her, I haven't been intimidated since about twelve.

"I hope ya got an army with ya, whoever you are," she said sternly.

Upon turning the rest of the way around to face the garden, I could see she had a large knife that I assumed she pulled from the basket. This one is full of surprises. I will make sure this one is fun. As I write, I begin feeling the sexual energy rising with the thought of my knife entering her body.

November 11, 1865

I did not move up to knives and the like until my twelfth year in the hellhole.

"He must be some sort of mute, we guess," said the constable to Ms. Applegum.

And in her sweetest voice she could muster, she said, "I am sure we will find out what his name is, isn't that correct, my little muffin?" She then pinched my cheek, and I could only wonder what smell had just invaded my nose.

"Yes, well, Ms. Applegum, can you please sign for the John Doe?" the constable asked.

"Yes, Yes. We have plenty of room for our little Muffin," she glared at me.

I looked away from her evil stare. After getting settled in, I went to lunch. I had not eaten at all that day in the constable station. I first met Jeremiah there, at the orphanage's cafeteria. Because I was new, that day was my turn to be deprived of the damn near meatless sandwich I was served every day for lunch the whole two years I was there.

He came into the café and stood behind me.

"Oi, Muva', is sis the muffin 'ats new?" he asked Applegum.

"Yes, Jeremiah. Treat him well," she said, walking down the aisle across from me. There were only about ten children total at the orphanage.

"So 'ee's the one wot's not got a voice, eh?" he asked.

"Yes, son. But again, treat him well," she said.

He leaned over and showed his grey teeth between those fat cheeks of his.

"I'm gonna treat ya well, I am. Trust me muffin, I'll have ya squealin' loik a wee lil piggy," he whispered in my ear, snatching my twice bitten sandwich from my hands.

"C'mon, Muffin. Beg for ya slop. SOOOEEE!!!!" he exclaimed.

The children all laughed as I reached for the sandwich out of hunger. This seemed to energize him into being more aggressive.

"Lemme hear ya squeal, piggy," he said, wagging the sandwich just out of my reach. He instantly knocked me to the ground when I tried to stand, but in the process, I hit my meal tray, splashing him with my water.

That made the other children laugh at him. Looking back, I think they were laughing so much because his focus wasn't on them. At this point, he was angry, and he raised me off the ground by my shirt with ease. Thanks to my good ole mother, though, I was used to abuse. After the third punch, I was sure I would black out.

"Smart one, are ya?" he said, drawing back for a fourth hit.

"That's enough son, I'm sure he's sorry, aren't you, Muffin?" the Bitch said.

"Take him to the infirmary. You were in a fight, little one, if the nurse asks and you decide to find your words." She gave me her trademark glare.

"Get up ya shitstain n' follow me," Jeremiah said and tossed me to the floor.

I was satisfied that I hadn't let out one yelp while he pummeled me. I crawled over to the bread and meat on the ground and The Bitch stepped on what was left and rapped my hand with that ruler of hers.

"I said to the infirmary, Muffin," she said.

Jerimiah grabbed my left arm. "Git up piggy. No lying around 'ere," he grunted.

After being shuffled down the long, hospital-like hall— which the children had to clean tirelessly—we arrived at the nurse's station where Nurse Henrietta kind of took care of us. After my second interaction with her, I realized that as long as Jeremiah kept her pockets full she would overlook anything that was done to us. Jeremiah made sure I watched as she gave him a hand job on my first visit with her.

No need to go into too much detail about how I learned to survive off the small amount of food I was given between my mother and Happy Sunshine Orphanage, or Horrible Stinky Orifice, as the children snickered about at bedtime.

December 2, 1865

A few weeks later, Ms. Applegum was happy they had increased the number in her stead to sixteen children. There was a black kid (or Tar-Baby, as Ms. Applegum would call him) that was tossed into the orphanage. I was eleven at the time of his arrival. He was placed in the bunk next to mine because all the other children would say that they did not want to be around a nigger, and I wouldn't talk. Only two days later, she came in, waking all the children.

"WAKE UP!!! WAKE UP, THE LOT OF YOU!!" she said, out of breath.

Everyone was groggy except Jake, the new boy. Unfortunately, that and his skin color instantly made him a target.

"WHICH ONE OF YOU LITTLE SNOT- NOSED, MUSHROOM-FACED CRIMINALS DID THIS!?" she screamed, holding up a half-eaten apple.

Jake began fidgeting, wiping his hands on the back of his nightshirt. If I were talking, I would have warned him that she sees everything. Her eyes instantly found their target.

"YOU!!! I knew you little niggers couldn't be trusted. C'mere!" she said, almost running to him.

She snatched his night pants and undergarments off. My rage began to build. Only because he had no chance and no kid would take the fall for him. She then began working him over with her trusted weapon.

"I'll teach you to steal from Happy Sunshine, you little twerp!" she yelled.

While he screamed and screamed, the other children cheered.

"Beat him. Beat the nigger!" they chanted, like some sick gospel song.

I finally could take no more. As she drew back to hit him again, I lunged at her right arm with a loud grunt and sunk my teeth into her arm as deep as I could. Her old, fat skin was surprisingly tissue thin, so much so that blood coursed from the bite and squished into my mouth. She let out a loud yelp and flung Jake into the radiator in between his and my bed with a loud crunch. The other kids were completely silent- in awe at this moment.

"You ungrateful, tar-baby loving piggy!" she yelled.

She was surprisingly strong and began punching my head. I finally released and dodged her fist grasp. I was so angry that I went back in, but this time on her upper right thigh. She screamed again, and then I realized that this wasn't such a good idea. Her ruler hand was now free, and she began striking me again.

Jake was now back up. Being nine, he may not have been as strong as me, but she was already off balance at this time and he used his entire body to topple her. She fell with a satisfying thud! Jake fell with her, but I snatched him under my bed as she clawed at his feet. I was losing my anger at this point and had not thought of an escape plan. I looked for Jake and he was gone.

"Muffin, over here!" he whispered.

Following his voice, I found he was under the bed next to me. I scurried over and rolled by the unlocked open door to our sleeping quarters. We ran down the hall and Jake was fast- barefoot with no pants or underwear on. I didn't know where he was leading me, and based on how he was pushing doors, he didn't either. By now, I could hear Applegum was up.

"Get back 'ere, ya lil bastards!" she sputtered, losing any proper English she had.

He fumbled open kitchen door that she left unlocked.

"In here," he whispered.

We hid behind the utensils, and of course, all the knives were locked away and out of reach, but there was plenty of food. I had a red film over my vision. I went to wipe my eyes and realized I was bleeding. Jake must have realized it when I did.

"Yore bleedin,' mate!" he exclaimed, still whispering with a fearful look in his eyes.

I looked around and Jake winced when he sat down. I found a washrag on the edge of the large porcelain sink and wiped my head and face.

"Thanks for the assist, mate; she's a monster," Jake said. I nodded emphatically.

I pointed to the apples on the floor across from us. Jake laughed. As hard as we worked, we could at least enjoy the reward. We had at least four or five apples before she barged in and grabbed both of us.

"You won't be bitin anyone anymore, Muffin," she said, glaring at me.

December 22, 1865

For the next two weeks, Applegum kept me in a pissy, padded room of the third wing, away from everyone. I received old porridge from breakfast at night. I'm sure a few times I heard Jeremiah spit in it.

"Where's ya lil spear-chucking thief to help you now?" he would laugh. "Don't worry; he's taken care of. I'm teachin' 'im very well, trost me!" he said, rubbing his crotch.

I didn't understand at that time what he meant.

In the middle of the night, on what I guess was a Wednesday, I began to hear the pitter-patter of child's feet. There were eight rooms on the wing I was on. I wasn't sure who it could have been, but I hadn't eaten in days, so I was delirious. Then—

"Psst! Muffin, ya down 'ere?" I instantly recognized Jake's voice. It sounded tired and energetic at the same time- if that was possible.

I crawled to the door and stuck my fingers through the opening of the food tray gate. His footsteps plodded faster, closing in on the last room I was located in. He grabbed my fingers softly with his cool, wet fingers and crouched to look at me eye to eye through the gate. His face was purple with bruises and cuts and his eye was swollen shut. When he smiled, he had teeth missing. I started crying at the sight of him.

"Ah, go on, most 'o the pains left, guvna," he said.

I had never taken the time to realize that Jake was very mature for his age.

"Lookie 'ere, brought ya some goo'ies ta pass the toime," he said, passing me a meaty sandwich and a few apples.

"I don't know 'ow long ya ta be unner restraint sos I would foind some way o' holdin' this stuff if I were ya. I'll bring summore when I get a chance. Ya holdin up awright palie?" he asked.

I fell in love with Jake at that point. He would be a brother forever to me and I would do whatever I could to get him out of this shitty place. I just needed to find a way to do so. I finished the sandwich and two of the apples and grunted and nodded. I held one of the apple cores up with a puzzled look on my face. The moonlight shining in from the opposite room kept enough light for us to see each other. I didn't know how he was able to get in and out of the sleeping quarters, let alone the kitchen.

"Daft. I survived a menny nights with these two beauts," he said, holding up two pieces of wire. "Wotch 'is."

He left my sight and I tried and follow him to no avail. I heard two clicks and the door opened. That was it. That was all we needed. I grunted and hugged him as tight as I could and kissed his forehead. I was near death and he barely knew me but came back for me. He pushed me off, snickering, as if I was some puppy.

"Awwright, awwright, mate. Great e'en't?" he asked me with a smile that was missing a few teeth.

I didn't care. I grabbed his hand and headed to the front, but he pulled away. I looked back, confused.

"Gettin' ahead of ya selv ain'tcha? We need a plan, mate. Applegum has gone and hired moor staff. And many 'r loik good ole Jeremiah, if not meana. This ain't the first place I've ran from, but this will be the worst, mate, I promise ya," he stated solemnly.

My rage began to build again. I clenched my fists and took my right thumb, slightly tilted my head back and dragged my thumbnail across my neck. Jake understood crystal clear. That night, Jake and I became best friends.

"There's no need ta commit murder. We just need ta get out ov 'ere, mate," he smiled sheepishly.

Jake paused because he knew I already had my mind made up. He bit a sandwich he had for himself, broke off half, and gave it to me.

"Look, Muffin, go on and sleep on it and I'll figure a way to hide sum food fa us and we can go. There's woods and trees and stuff and we'll never be found, okay? And wif out killin'! Ya murderin' bastard." He laughed, patting my back to head into the cell.

Jake never knew of my murdering tendencies and that made him so innocent to me. I hugged him again in the cell and tears formed at the bottom of my eyes.

He whispered, "we 'aven't got long now, Muffin. 'Keep ya 'ead up.' Is wot me mum would tell me, afore she was murdered and all."

I stepped away from him, shocked, and he closed the door. I crouched down and slid my fingers through the grate once more. He clasped my fingers, let go, and I listened to his little feet get to the end of the corridor where they paused. I assumed that he was looking for any of the new hires that were surely asleep by that time.

"Don't worry, I'll be back wif sumfin sweet next toime, mate. Maybe a muffin for ya, Muffin," he whispered back down the hallway.

I stuck my tongue through my lips to blow a raspberry and it echoed loudly. I heard him stifle a loud laugh. I listened until I no longer heard his feet.

The next evening, Jeremiah brought my porridge with a fly in it, and for the first time in my entire life, I smiled. I could not think about anything negative enough to take my smile away. I just could not wait to kill them all.

October 16, 1887

Tabitha finally went back inside humming after she placed her knife carefully back in her basket. She has no clue that her demise is close.

"Make it nice for me, my sweet." Sarah snarls.

"Oh I will my dear, trust me, I will," I whisper.

October 17, 1887

After finishing my day today, I went back to my original home and waited for nightfall. I took special precautions this time. I made sure many people saw me going in and out of my apartment at least twice. It took me almost until midnight to be comfortable enough to leave through my back window.

The walk to Tabitha's house is a short mile and a half. When I arrived, there were a few people on the street, but after a certain time it would not matter. A few moments later, the streets were empty. It was time for me to make my move. I took a paper that I had picked up, threw it into the trash barrel, and headed to her alley. I took a quick peek around and I pulled the makeshift lock pick from my pocket. The whole objective now was to remain as quiet as possible. Originally, when I was making my art pieces, I was unsure if I would use such a thing since I would be doing so on the streets. I heard the perfect clicking noise that let me know the lock was unhinged. I didn't have a clue if the gate squeaked or not, and I opened it just enough to squeeze through.

The garden was even more marvelous at night than during the day. The clear, moonlit sky reflected different colors in a melody of oranges, reds and greens. And the smells were very tantalizing now that I was closer. I almost wanted to pluck a tomato from the bushel. That was until Sarah showed me one decaying in front of my very eyes.

"Forgive me, deary," I whispered aloud.

I reached for the doorknob and it was already open— I pulled my hand away quickly. I instantly felt exposed, that is until I heard a loud crash upstairs. I dashed inside. I heard shouting from somewhere. I fumbled around in the dimly lit kitchen area and made my way down a small, short corridor to her home's stairs. I could tell that there was a large scuffle going on upstairs. I snuck as quietly as I could up the stairs, but it did not sound as though they would even stop if they could. I heard a man's voice saying something unclear to who I assumed was her. Her home was dark. I listened quietly.

"Eever ya' pay me or ya doi. Dose'r ya only two options," the man said. His voice was very deep and confident. He sounded as though he had been doing this for years.

Tabitha then sounded like one of Them. One of my victims.

"I'll pay ya not one pence for shit. I work fa no one now. I'ma free lady now. I won't be tricked anymoor." She laughed. The room where all this was going on was at the top of the stairs to the right. I saw a sliver of light coming out. Then I began to have second thoughts. I did not want to waste my artwork on a stupid man who was only following his instincts. But the preparation would all be for naught if I stopped then. I had a perfect spot that I would be taking her to in the sewers.

They were arguing too much to hear any creaks on the steps that I made. I slid around the top of the banister with my back against it in an effort to make myself as flat as possible. I did not wish to be seen just yet. I caught a glimpse of the man as I passed the crack in the door. He was tall and built like an ox. He looked as though he lived his life the way he was built. From what I saw, he was wearing a dirty tee shirt with his arms exposed and matted slacks. His head was as bald as mine, and he had sunburned skin. His arms were the size of tree trunks.

I slipped to the side wall of the door and gave myself a moment to think. I glanced around in the darkness and saw Sarah looking at me. Her skin was sunken, as though she had not eaten in weeks. She floated past me and stood in front of the door. As quietly as possible I whispered, "We can find another."

She cackled and placed both hands on the front of the door. An odd, grayish purple light emitted from the palms of her hands and the door whooshed open, startling Tabitha's unwanted guest. Sarah disappeared with a shriek that was only heard by me.

"Bloody bullocks!" the man shouted in surprise.

I could only assume this gave Tabitha her chance to attack, as I heard footsteps and a loud crash.

"Oi, so ya plan to pay off ya debts wif ya loife then, bitch?" he laughed.

I then heard a loud slap and she yelped. Then, the familiar sounds of bedsprings, and Tabitha began to make choking noises. He was doing it wrong. If this ogre was killing her, he was using his bare hands and he would ruin all that I have worked for. I broke the corner to the door and saw the room was a mess. There were broken picture frames and all sorts of figurines on the floor. The bed was in shambles as the lummox was on top of her. I instantly saw Sarah and good ole Edgar and the room became a blur of redness. His hands were around her throat, squeezing the life from her. Her good eye was red and leaking while her bad one was staring into my soul again. Her smooth, full lips were purple. She was trying to claw at his face and keep air in her lungs, but her struggles were increasing.

I had no time to think. My heart was making the sound of running elephants in my chest. I reached into my cloak and pulled out my six-inch blade. I needed to be quick about this, as I needed her alive. The man realized that someone else was in the room. I reached around his shoulders and gave him two quick gashes in his throat. Blood erupted from his throat in a red fountain. He released her and grabbed his throat as though he was trying to choke himself now. Tabitha's face was now a red mask and she began to cough. His gurgles were pleasing sounds to me. I laughed hysterically at his reaction.

I began my celebration too early and I was too close to him. I cannot believe that I have not learned this.

December 29, 1865

Jake and I spoke the last few days while I was in confinement. We laughed about Applegum's howls the night I bit her. After my second week, I was reunited with the regular kids who accepted the abuse. The children would call me 'Nigger lover' and other derogatory names. One—Billy, the orphanage bully—actually spat on me and Jeremiah laughed. None of these things bothered me. Jake and I barely got sleep at night for we were going over different avenues and methods of escape. I felt sorry for him because I still did not wish to speak. Our conversations would consist of my pointing and grunting while he would agree or disagree.

Jake and I became inseparable during this time. We would always sit together at mealtime. This made the other children jealous. He whispered things and then laughed at my silly grunts. He and I would trade foods and play games that only two people could play. It had gotten so bad that Applegum and her cohorts separated us at bedtime. But, even on these nights he would plod to my bunk. We would still find time to have fun. Some nights I would feign sleep and pretend to try and scare him. He would go along with it unless something had been on his mind, such as a kid bothering him or a change in the plans for escape.

Unfortunately, the latter was not a plan of escape for me. For me, it was a plan of attack. So, when he would talk, I would nod and act as though I was listening. At these times, my eyes were always on the chemicals under the sink in the kitchen. They were never locked away. The only thing was, I was pissed that I could not read. I hated it. But, I knew they weren't for us to eat or drink. My mother taught me that.

During one of our meetings, I pointed to the knives.

"C'mon, mate, I tol ya we don't need 'em dead. I jus want out!" he would say every time.

See, Jake was a very smart kid. Almost too smart. He had not taught me to pick the locks yet. He knew that my mind was set on those utensils. Our meeting spot was always in the kitchen unless one of Applegum's new guards were awake. If that were the case, we would stay in the sleeping quarters. During this time, I would watch ever so closely as Jake picked the locks. I had to lie to my little brother and it hurt me to do so. Jake's small mind would not understand. These monsters were an infection and allowing them to live was impossible. At eleven and a half, I knew this, and at nine, Jake had tears in his eyes anytime I talked about it.

Jeremiah knew that the way to set me off was by bothering Jake. That was the only thing I hated about my friendship with Jake. I would stop any new child who came to the orphanage who would begin to pick on Jake due to his race and size. My height and silence made me a mystery and a threat automatically.

Now, Jake had planned the whole escape for us the night before my 'birthday'. He explained that he had done it this way because there were not as many orderlies working that night. And, we could quietly escape through the underground sewage tunnels. At breakfast, we discussed how we were going to leave. He said he had a months' worth of food stashed near the escape route. He had not known this, but I was not ready. I wanted as many people there as possible. For what I had planned, Jeremiah had to be there. And, he was off that night. I knew for a fact that he would be there the next day because it was chicken and gravy night. He would pay for what he had done to my brother's face. Looking back, I wished that we had left when Jake was ready.

That night, he came over to my bed and shoved me.

"Awwright, Muffin, let us depart from deez whoite walls," he said.

I kept my eyes closed and didn't move. We both knew he couldn't make this journey without me. Now his whisper sounded upset.

"Oi, sleepy 'ead! No toime fa jokes, mate. I awready checked, ever' ones asleep loike babes. Get up now; let's go!" He pushed me with more force this time. Then, a concerned, "Mate!"

I opened my eyes, holding back possible tears. I shook my head, 'No,' and did my negative grunt. Jake's eyes told me everything that I needed to know. He had begun to feel betrayed at this point.

"Not now, mate. We got'a go!" He did not whisper his last statement and he had a complete look of confusion on his face.

A child began to stir next to my bunk and he crouched down.

"Mate, wot's this, then, eh? Ya fink o' me as too scared ta make this trip on me own, do ya? Coz I'll do it. Woteveah, ya got planned, let it go, mate," he whispered.

This is when I realized that Jake was smarter than the average nine-year-old was. I turned over so not to face him. I could no longer hold back my tears and I did not want him to see me crying.

"Muffin, Ya con't be serious roight now, half o' these tossers aren't as daft as ya fink they are and nowhere near as guilty. I mean you and me, we got 'em beat, we do. The toime is now. Let's go, mate." The urgency in his voice was now unmistakable and I felt the tears creating a puddle on my pillow. He began to fully shake my bed and tried to pull me out of it.

Billy sat up from across the room.

"Oi, ken you und ya lilo nigger girlfriend take 'at luv shite down tha hool? Sum ov us are troin ta sleep, we are!" he yelled. It echoed throughout the sleeping quarters.

Jake had no choice but to plod his little feet back to his bunk. As he passed, I turned back so he and I would not lock eyes. I felt his piercing stare. I had to keep my sobs as quiet as possible while I cried that night.

I awoke earlier than usual that morning before breakfast. Today was my 'birthday'. They had no real record of my birthday at Happy Sunshine. They would only go off the perverse idea that a year after I arrived, I was eleven. Jake did not sit next to me that morning. He had not looked at me at all. I was slightly hurt by this, but I knew he would not understand why we couldn't leave until that night. For the first time since I had been at Happy Sunshine, I was happy to see Jeremiah. He went over to Billy and whispered to him. They both looked at Jake and sneered. I saw red.

I found out that I had kitchen duty before lunch and was pleased. During lunch, they prepped for dinner as well. There was a huge icebox in the kitchen that was all but impossible to get out of if you were caught on the inside of it. I cleaned the kitchen as slowly as I could, waiting for the correct time to make my move. Our cook finally went into the icebox and I closed the door behind him and grabbed the bleach. I poured as much as I could into the gravy without changing the smell. I could hear him still fumbling with the door, knowing that he could not get it open. I took this time to get two knives from the cabinet and then opened the door. He came out and grabbed my shoulder.

"Oi' c'mere, ya lilo runt. I could've doied in 'ere, dya know that?" he said, throwing me to the ground.

I felt one of the knives cut my upper thigh. I ran back to the sleeping area, changed my bloody pants, and placed the knives into my pillowcase.

I smiled because Jake had no clue I would make up the previous night to him.

We got to lunch, and my brother still wasn't talking to me. I sat at a table by myself and hoped he would look at me, but he didn't. At that moment, Billy walked to him, took his milk, and poured it over him.

"I've never seen a zebra nigger before," he laughed.

I grew to hate that term and anyone who felt comfortable using it. I ran over to Billy before he reacted, grabbed his tray and smacked him to the floor with it. The entire café went into an uproar. I climbed Billy and pounded his face bloody with the hard plastic tray. Jeremiah finally grabbed me and pinned me into the closest wall. He kicked Jake away just in case.

"Yoo two won't gang up on me loike ya got me mum, you won't," he said, scowling.

Applegum stood up from her table. "Take him away, Son. And give him his present now for his birthday." She smiled with her grey teeth.

He got me to the padded rooms, back to the last cell, and closed the door behind him. He unbuckled his pants and my anger instantly left. I did not know what he was doing.

"Toime ta show ya what I did ta ya nigger's hole, boy," he said, grabbing me by my shoulders.

I punched him as hard as I could and he laughed. He slapped me to the ground and mounted me. He then pulled down my trousers and said "Happy Birfday." As he entered me, I cried out for the first time in two years. I blacked out at that time. When I came to, he was lifting his trousers.

"Don't worry Muffin, I'll come and get ya fore ya birfday dinna," he snickered.

My bottom hurt so badly that I could barely stand, but I could only think of Jake. I needed to warn him before dinner. Jeremiah headed to the door and my rage made me want to say something to him, so I opened my mouth and the words felt like glass in my vocal chords as they left my lips.

"Ya…doie…today!" was all I could muster. I was exhausted.

"Bullocks, well look atcha, Muffin. Ya ken speak afta all. I con't wait ta tell mum I cured anova one," he laughed.

She ordered him to do this to me and whoever else in there. I remember being thirsty at that time and it wasn't just for water. Her blood was the only thing that would fully quench my thirst.

I walked out and began to look for my brother. I knew I had time, but now I could speak. I found Jake cleaning the beds in the sleeping quarters and limped to him.

"Muffin? Wot's on ya, mate?" he asked as I fell into him. "Thanks fa the save at lun--" When he heard me speak he peed himself.

"No…eet…dinna." I cut him off and continued. "Be…re'ee…" I held up three fingers. "…ours," I finished.

In my mind, my throat was possibly bleeding. We had a bathroom in the sleeping area to keep children from having accidents. I ran to the bathroom and guzzled water from the spout. Jake followed behind me with wet trousers. He smiled with his missing teeth.

"I fought ya wer broke, mate!" he cried happily. "But I gotcha, I won't eet tha food and we're out ov 'ere in free 'ours, but 'ow?" he asked, confused.

After I gulped my last bit of water, my throat was in less pain, but my anus was screaming. This angered me and I felt no urge to explain. My words did not make any sense in my head. I grabbed him by his shirt.

"No eet!!" I said once again and looked directly into his eyes.

"Okay, mate. Just take 'er easy rioto?" He understood everything at that point.

At dinner, Applegum always made sure we would eat together as a sick sort of 'family.' The cook had gone home and Jeremiah was serving us in his place. I had grabbed the two blades from my pillowcase after my conversation with Jake earlier. Upon receipt of my tray, I kept my eyes on Jeremiah. I really wanted him first. Ms. Applegum received her extra helping of food and sat down. Another rule she had was that we could not eat until Jeremiah was there. And on the night in question, that was perfectly fine. My brother and I would be walking out of there with no worries. Jake sat next to me and was extra fidgety. I now know that he does that when he's nervous.

Jeremiah came from behind the kitchen with his large plate and sat next to his mother. He began to dig in, and before he could put the food in his mouth, she popped his hand.

"We must say grace first, Son," she said.

After she said grace for everyone, she gave the order to begin eating. I watched as everyone did as he was told. Jake leaned on my shoulder and began to cry when he saw the first child's face balled up. I shushed him as best as I could. I kept my eyes fixed on Jeremiah. I wanted to see his reaction the most. He then locked eyes with me. He looked at my tray and knew it was too late at that moment. He had already eaten more than half of his plate. When he looked at his mother, she had begun coughing and reaching for her water. It would do nothing for her and I knew it. Billy cried out as he started vomiting. I almost laughed then. I looked at Jake who now was looking around at the chaos and was crying. I softly slapped him back to reality.

"I tolya,...Muffin! I...din't...wont this. Why did jah afta do this?" he was almost telling me through his tears.

"Get stoff an' pick tha frunt lock," I said to him. After two years of not talking, I surprised myself at my ability to form complete thoughts.

He looked up at me for a few seconds, nodded, and then ran off. I made sure he was gone and pulled one of the knives from the waistband of my pants. I stood up and passed by the children whose bodies could not take the poison too well. Some had fallen from their seats, some of them had their faces planted in their trays, others still were crawling around on the ground looking for I don't know what. I walked over to Applegum and Jeremiah, who were both incapacitated. Applegum's breathing had become labored. I was her height when she sat down. Yet I sat down next to her-facing her.

"Me name ain't Muffin, bitch," I said, stabbing her in her thigh.

She let out a small, raspy, wheezy sound as the knife penetrated her flesh. It was music to my ears at the time. She had a look on her face as though she had known this day was coming.

"M…m..a..ma…ma…" I heard Jeremiah behind her, bubbling out between his gurgles.

"Oi, don't cha fink I forgot about ya, Jeremiah. One atta toime, me, boy," I said, getting up from my seat in front of Applegum.

I walked over to him with a smirk on my face. I could not help myself. I reached into my pants, pulled out the second knife, and stabbed him in his privates. He let out a mumbled 'Uhh' when the knife went in. Again, it made me smile. When I did this, I heard a loud scream from the entrance to the Café. I looked over and it was Jake. I was so angry; this was what I did not want him to see.

"WOT ARE YA DOIN' BAC 'ERE?" I screamed at him. That caused pain in my throat again.

"Wot's wrong wifya, Muffin?" he cried back to me. Snot had begun to flow from his nose now and he had a sack on his shoulder.

"Key," I said to him. Ms. Applegum had a master key that she carried around her neck. I quickly ran over to her to retrieve it from her. As I searched her neck for the key, she brought her hand up and clasped it on *mine. I removed the knife from her thigh and stabbed through her wrist and she released me. Jake cried out again.*

"STOP IT! STOP IT, MUFFIN-- LET'S JOST GET OUTTA 'ERE!" he shouted, balling.

I found the key and began walking with him. I gave him the key and nodded for him to go on to the front door. I had one last thing to do. I got to the supply closet and found lantern oil and matches. I grabbed three of the almost filled lanterns, cracked one against a wall, and rolled it down the floor of the Café hard enough so it broke against the back wall. I lit the other two and threw one of them inside. I watched as the oil ignited on some of the children's clothing. I think that I saw one of the child's eyes explode when the fire got too hot.

I turned to walk out and Jeremiah was standing at the door. He had blood all over the front of his pants.

"And where do yoo fink yore goin,' muffin? Ya gotta go bac in dat 'ole inna back," he said, almost falling over.

I could not believe he was able to stand. I walked around him, just out of his reach. I walked until my back was facing the door, threw the last lantern at him, and laughed as the flames engulfed his body. He was too weak to scream. I stood and watched. I learned that lantern oil was a slow burn from watching him. NOW was my time to leave. I made it to the front door and on my way I grabbed three more lanterns, poured more oil, and lit it to make sure the whole damn building burned. Jake's eyes were swollen from crying. He had already opened the front door and I picked up the heavy sack of food he had prepared for us. When I got outside, we walked around the back and there was nothing but large trees and woods around us. I pulled his hand and he snatched it away from me. After we had gotten a few steps into the deep woods, he dropped his sack and began punching me in the chest.

"Yore a monsta,' Muffin. A BLOODY MONSTA'!!" he screamed at me.

I followed my first instinct and knocked him down. He looked up at me and wiped his tears and nose. I loved my brother and I would have done it all over again if I needed to. I knew he would never understand that this was the payment and they had deserved every cent of it. I picked him up and hugged him to my chest- all the while he fought until I spoke.

"No more Muffin. Me name's Troy. I luv ya, Jake. An' I din't wont ya ta see all dat, but tha toimin' was wot caused ya ta be at the wrong place when it all 'appened. But I won't do it again. I promise ya that," I said to him, holding him close to me.

At that age, I did not know that promises were easily broken.

October 17, 1887

He moved a lot faster than I expected for someone who had been stabbed in the neck twice. He reached for my throat, but only got my collar while trying to lift me from the ground. I am no huge fellow, but I am no slouch either. We tussled for a moment, but he had no good grasp on me. Combined with his loss of blood, he would never have moved me. He toppled to his knees, taking short gasps. His hand fell from his neck and there were only a few pumps as his heart had begun to run out of its life water. I realized that I was holding my breath. I let out a long sigh, placed my hands on my knees and bent over.

I tried to recover to take care of her next. Her voice was dry, cracked and hoarse, all at the same time.

"Hel-help...me...ack...Thomas," she said.

But I was surprised. *Help her with what?* I began to ponder. I just did help her.

"Th—the body; we have to bury....the body...garden!" she sputtered, getting off the bed. Full of surprises, she is.

For some reason, I rushed to her aid. I saw that the dresser was actually still intact, but she was about to fall back into it. Not that I didn't completely believe her, but I needed to test her to make sure this wasn't some sort of accident.

"Shouldn't we obtain a constable?" I asked, looking into her good eye, which was still red, but no longer tearing.

She instantly regained control. "NO!! Please Thomas, no constables!" she cried, terrified.

I was confused. If this man came to attack her, why wouldn't she want to get a constable?

"We need to clean up this mess and dispose of 'is body," she said.

I laughed in my head.

"C'mon, mate, we need to move," she said, running to her bathroom. She came back with rags soaked in bleach and began scrubbing the floor.

"Well c'mon, ge' a moove on. Wrap that boe'ee up in that rug, there," she said, out of breath.

I had to smile as I began to stuff and roll the behemoth into the rug she pointed to. His body was heavy and moved all over the place and where I didn't want it to go. I had never had to reposition one this size before, even as an assistant mortician. She squatted down by his head and assisted me with rolling his body. With her as close to me as she was, I saw that she was very beautiful. I saw all the freckles on her face and it was cute to me. She had a lot of sweat accumulating around her breast area and I was trying to ignore it, but it was difficult. Between killing this lummox and her fucking secrets, I am not as pleased with killing her as I was earlier. I licked my lips and tried to ignore what was happening in my pants.

"Ee's a big one, 'ee is," she said, breaking the silence.

"Tabitha, what the hell is going on here?" I asked, sounding concerned.

"Now's not the tiome, ya bloke. We'll 'ave it out after we clean this all up. Trust me, I got questions foreya as well," she stated, nodding to me to do one more roll.

For some reason, she seemed to know this all too well. She jumped up and whooshed past me to run downstairs for something. I only knew this because she called back up to me.

"Thomas, please be a dear and finish woiping up the red stoff, will ya?" she yelled up to me.

Inexplicably, this was making me more and more attracted to her. I got on my knees, removed my gloves and had just begun the process when I saw a pair of grey, bony feet floating in front of me just near the body. This made me pause, knowing who it was and what she wanted. But, as I watched her feet, I saw the odd purple-gray aura around it. The same color aura that I witnessed when she shoved the door open. What made it odd was that there was another black aura coming from the man's body and it flowed to her feet. The aura around her became brighter for a few seconds and then subsided. I heard Tabitha's footsteps and could tell she was upset at what she saw, because in a stern voice she said: "GIT A MOOVE ON THOMAS, WHAT'S GOT YA INNA BOIND!?!"

"S-sorry; I was caught up in something. What did you need us to do?" I asked as if I didn't know what was next.

"Well, let's get these on 'im and we will get 'im down to me garden, dig a 'ole and put 'im in. Simple math, mate," she quickly responded, pulling a ball of twine from her pocket.

She tied the top of the rug, the victim's neck, and his feet with a nice firm knot. She squatted down and gave me the "Let's go" look, so I squatted as well.

"Off we go now, guvna!" she said with a loud grunt as we lifted the wrapped body onto our shoulders. I walked backwards down the stairs with her attacker. She kept a cadence that was comfortable for the both of us. We got him into the garden under the high, clear, starless night sky. The moon provided the perfect lighting for what needed to be handled. We dropped the body by an area that she chose. There were beautiful tomatoes growing from this area. She went over into the darkness of a dusty, rust covered shamble of a shed and I heard the creaking noise of a door opening. Then silence. She finally emerged with a large spade. Kind of like the one I used on one of my earlier victims. She then shoved it into my hand.

"Yore boe'ee, yore 'hole. Start diggin'!" she whispered as loud as possible.

I was compelled to obey. I hated to destroy the tomatoes- so much so that she had to dig them up before I started to work. I dug for hours, until she said it was fine. We placed the body into the ground, face up, and before we began placing the dirt on it, I could have sworn the body already looked decayed. We finished burying the remains and re-soiled the area. She seems very different than I assumed. I could tell she was aroused. After burying this man who had just tried to kill her, she grabbed my face and said:

"Kiss me under the moonlight, darling; it has long since been a fantasy of mine."

And before I could say anything she kissed me. I did nothing to stop her.

October 21, 1887

Tabitha has been in love with me since the moment she laid her good eye on me. She told me that sitting on her stoop today.

"You did not realize that I was looking for you almost every other day, did you?" she asked me.

"Not at all," I replied.

But I did. I did not realize how much she was into me, but I knew that she had been looking for me. Tabitha does not mind too much that I am quiet. She asks why, but tells me it is likeable. It's like the more things that I don't tell her, the more aroused she gets. Whenever we are intimate, no matter how hard we go at it, she always yells for me to go "harder" and "faster." I pull her hair and bite her in all sorts of sensitive places. And it's like the more violent it is, the harder she orgasms.

One day, I arrived and she was eating cheese and fruit on her bed with a carving board and knife. We started our sexual routine, I behind her with her crouched over in a dog position, when suddenly she took my hand from her hair and placed the knife in it.

"UUUNUUUNGHH....I want you to cut me loike ya cut that bugger trying to kill me," she moaned like a whimpering dog. I slowed down my strokes, looking at the knife. In the shiny blade's reflection, I saw Sarah behind me.

"I—I c-can't do th-that," I stuttered through wheezes of excitement.

"Yes you can my sweet, right under my breast, right here," she said, reaching back to my right wrist and guiding it to her right breast.

I snatched away. My erection had grown and my sexual mind was in a frenzy!! Her skin is so smooth. She has red freckles all over her body, including her breasts. I felt all the urges that sent me on my path in the first place begin to fill my head. I held the knife over my head, biting my bottom lip, and thought about entombing it into the back of her neck. Sarah was yelling at me *"Do it! For me! Do it now!"*

I threw the knife and grabbed her by her throat. Burying her face into the pillow, I began to give her thunderous strokes. She began to cry out in pain and ecstasy all at once. Through the muffles, I heard her screaming at the top of her lungs:

"YEEESSSS!!! CHOKE MEE!!! CHOKE MEEEEEE!!!"

I began screaming to the point that we both climaxed. I thrusted as hard as I could into her, feeling the last of my energy and seed percolate into her. I fell back while she stayed in her bent, dog-like position. She was leaned over to where her breasts were touching her upper thigh.

Tabitha has a perfect body. She looks almost angelic. But the things we do in bed make her soo evil to me. And this instance wasn't the worst of them. Her long, blackish silver hair was stuck to her face through the sweat and clung to her body as she heaved. She whimpers sometimes after we finish.

"That....was...amazing, my dear," she said.

Tabitha knows how to make me feel like a man. I don't know what is going on between her and me, but I have no choice but to fall for her. See, the only thing I feel wild about is that I am actually cheating on Sarah. But, hadn't she done the same to me with Edgar? It doesn't bother me that she watches as Tabitha and I have our way with each other. In fact, it excites me some nights. All she does is hiss at me and plague my dreams. She can do nothing in reality, though, so I enjoy it.

It's funny that Tabitha has a green thumb as well. She is a teacher amongst other things, but she does not always get into it. We both have skeletons in our closets and I know mine will be harder to expose. I found out that she was a pitiable child. She had no real parenting. I find so many things like these, and she loves to tell them to me. But I never tell her my past. There is never time, for one, because she walks me to the edge of my route and I leave and never tell her a thing. I feel that that is what has to happen. She need not know about the death and carnage that I'm made of. So I will be silent about it. But, every once and a while, I spend the night. On these nights, I'm not silent.

October 23, 1887

I was sitting in a large room at the head of a large table. There were five chairs with five of my victims on either side of the table. Everyone was dressed in formal evening attire. Ms. Applegum was seated in the first chair to my left, and across from her was her mindless son. Beside him was one of the prostitutes that I hacked up, and across from her was the first one I did after going to the tavern with Jim. At the other end of the head of the table was my mother. She, along with the others, were laughing uncontrollably. It was dark in the room. Almost pitch black, and the only thing keeping it from being so were the five candles in line on the middle of the large, oval, marble table.

They laughed until my mom stood up with a plate. Everyone was quiet and looking at me with piercing stares. She walked toward me with the plate. A very unintelligible smile was on her face, showing more than a normal number of teeth, which had grown all over each other. As she got closer, I began to make out steak and mashed potatoes on the plate. Nausea settled in at the site of them. I looked at her, she smiled, and her face warped into Sarah's. But, she sounded like my mother.

"Eat up, ya little shit. I made it special for you. Lick the plate clean," she said.

I looked up at her and shook my head, "No"." For some reason, I couldn't speak. I looked down the table to the right and Jeremiah was there.

"C'mon, Muffin. I helped 'er make it faya," he said with a smirk and blood dribbling from his teeth.

"Yeah, Muffin. It's time to eat your food," Ms. Applegum said. I looked across the table from Jeremiah and saw her speaking to me.

The table burst into flames and Tabitha was on it, screaming, while they started laughing again. Then suddenly, the table stopped burning and they started cutting chunks off her body with knives and forks. Her body was shaking with each lump they took off. She didn't scream because her mouth was welded shut with her own skin. My last two female victims from Scotland Yard were eating her toes. And when they finished, Tabitha's grey eye came rolling down the table to me, and I jumped up, knocking the plate from Sarah's hand. It landed on the table and the oily black substance from my previous dream appeared from inside of the potatoes.

I looked back at Sarah, and she still had a warped smile with those teeth that were large and didn't belong in her mouth but on different animals. When I looked back at the people at the table, Applegum and Jeremiah were charcoal black with leathery, sticky skin. The only thing that I could make out was their eyes looking at me. But, they were still laughing, and the women had the injuries that I caused.

The table disappeared below us into a gigantic hole of darkness, and at the center of the hole was Tabitha's eye. The hole of darkness began to swirl and brought things toward it. It sucked in the two prostitutes first. Then, the Applegum family, but Sarah was standing there smiling that hideous, toothy grin. I looked down and the edge of the marble floor was gone. My feet were on the precipice of the black swirling hole. Her eyes were now gone, and the swirling thing at my feet replaced them. I looked back down and there were black smoky hands coming from the hole and grabbing me. The fingers were long and gnarly. I turned and held onto the chair to keep them from taking me in. Sarah was standing over me with her grin and huge teeth while the swirls in her eyes continued to spin. She had everyone's voice that was previously at the table when she spoke.

"Was it good? Did you like it? TELL US YOU LIKED IT!!!! I LIKED IT!!! WE ALL LIKED IT!!!" the voices said, louder and louder.

I was being pulled into the darkness and it felt cold to my feet. I was now hanging on to the arms of the chair and my ankles were in the darkness. Something felt as though it was gnawing on my feet. She then plucked my hands from the chair's arms.

I wake up screaming on many nights from these dreams that I do not want to see any more of. Sarah is becoming more and more impatient. Tabitha says nothing. She's right there for me, wiping sweat of my head and humming and kissing me like a child. She tells me all sorts of things to take my mind off the dreams. One night, after one of these episodes, she asked:

"Who is Sarah?" with a straight face.

I looked away from her and sat on the edge of the bed. I didn't know what to say because I wanted to tell her it was Ms. Applegum. But it was like her eye was aware enough to look through my soul. I was afraid to tell her anything. I see that eye as a dangerous tool but also as if it were a light for a moth. I never lie to her face.

"I don't know," I lied, walking to the window.

Tabitha does not ever question me. If I lie and she knows it, she will not call me on it. It's as if she likes to be treated the way I treat her. She seems to like pain. I know this sounds crazy, but I don't think she knows how to operate without it.

"You were asking her to stop in your sleep." She pried more.

"I said I don't know." I lied again. And she knew.

Some days, I walk past her home and she runs out to get me to stop. I tell her that I assumed she'd be asleep or that she was gone to the market. She does not understand that I have another creature all-together that is on my case. Sarah does not allow me to have a good night's rest unless Tabitha and I have an intense sexual romp. I am torn between them. So, I'm deciding to focus on Tabitha and see if there is anything that she can say or do to put me back on my path.

"What happened to your eye?" I boldly asked after one of our sweaty escapades.

"The time isn't right, dear. In due time, I will fill you in on all my secrets," she laughed, snuggling close to me.

"But I do wan'na know one thing, dear. Three weeks ago, when Baggins came to me 'ome and ya stabbed 'im rioght proper loike, rememba?" she asked in her broken language.

I was instantly nervous.

"Yes, I remember," I stated, hiding my nervousness.

"Wot were you doin' 'ere? Loike, I don't rememba you sayin' anyfing to me that week an' outta the blue there ya were. The roight place at the roight toime. What were ya plans and why were ya carryin' a knife?" she asked.

Sweat began to form on my palms and my throat felt dry. I didn't know if it was from the intimacy or from her question. I needed time to think on this. I had not even thought that she would come back to that situation because she was happy with where things were. I had no clue what to say. But, Sarah did.

"I was walking past and I thought about knocking on your door when I heard a loud amount of ruckus. When I tried the front door and it was locked, I went around back. At that time, I had not known about your garden and was wondering what was going on. I had a feeling you were in danger and went up. I only had the knife because there have been so many killings going on as of late, and I did not want to fall victim to the animal," I said to her.

"Hmmm..." she said questionably.

All I could think was that that blasted eye had done its job and made me out to be a liar. If she did not believe me, then I would have tightened my grip around her neck and killed her right here.

"Well, the way ya handled ole Baggins, some could say yew were the murderer," she replied.

I didn't push anymore.

October 27, 1887

I was walking up to Tabitha's home today when I saw two seedy characters coming from her back fence. One was a short, stocky man wearing a brown plaid hat with a vest and white dress shirt. The second was a female and I already knew she was the brains of this operation. She was wearing a black vest over a red evening jacket and a tall red hat with a black velvet strip across. Everything she was wearing was custom made. I walked past as though I did not see them, and they didn't see me. I tried to listen to as much of their conversation as possible. What I did see, when she reached up to grab the man's face, was that she had a shiny pistol on her hip.

"I'm sure 'at's where the whore livs. I'm omost positiv," the short, stocky man said.

"Listen, Yarney, I am tired of going to these different homes to no avail. If you morons don't find my brother, I promise you, they won't find you," she said, releasing his cheeks.

The man Yarney replied and I was too far away to hear what he said. Who the fuck were they talking about? Baggins? Tabitha didn't tell me anything. I didn't ask anything either. I needed to find out who these people were. I went around the edge of the bend and posted up near an abandoned building. I watched as the well-dressed woman in red fussed at Yarney a while longer. She then walked to an expensive carriage, leaving Yarney to stand watch. He lit a fag and continued to wait out front for her. "Where is she," I wondered? If he tried to do anything to her, he would have died there and sloppily. We waited. I was at least thirty to forty paces away from the stocky Yarney. My surprise would have been my advantage. See, advantage is everything in any situation. I remember the man who taught me this lesson- he's the one whose name I use to this day.

March 2, 1866

"*M*ake a decision, son. Whether it's right or wrong, make a decision and stick behind it," he would say while we sat on the back porch playing chess.

Well, wait; allow me to go back, I am getting ahead of myself. Jake and I had gone on for months, deeper and deeper into the woods. Things worsened when we began to run out of food. We had to try and hunt things, but what did we, two children, nine and twelve, know about foraging and hunting? There were all sorts of animals and wildlife that we ran into. We became just as savage while those months passed.

Jake and I learned to communicate with grunt and whistles. I had to teach him certain grunts and what they would mean at what times. He actually taught me how to whistle and what we could do while far away to indicate how bad the danger was. But, Jake would always find times for us to talk. For Jake, talking was second nature while for me it was the opposite. Nevertheless, Jake was my brother and I never denied him after the orphanage incident. Mistakenly, I had only taken two knives, which we used to cut through trees while finding our way around or to cut off some of the food and things that we had with us. I just wished that we had thought things through a lot better.

"We got plen'ee ov toime ta foind moore people," Jake would tell me.

I would nod in approval. So as children, what did we do? Eat until we were full every night. We thought two pence of conservation. We brought no pots or pans with us. We just knew these two sacs we carried from Happy Sunshine were perfect. I kept the matches from the fire and lit fifteen fires until they got wet in a rainstorm. After that, Jake would not allow me to eat anything I killed. See, whenever we would catch something, say a frog or squirrel, we would need to cook it right then. Jake had read somewhere that if the animals were not cleaned and gutted, the meat would be spoiled and we would become sick. I didn't believe him. Either way, I would cook the food fast so he wouldn't be upset or start crying. We would continue for hours, days and weeks looking for civilization.

"Yore gonna get sick," he would say with tears in his eyes when he saw me with fresh meat. I now realize that he needed me alive as much as I needed him alive.

"Pleeze Troy, don't eat it. Pleeze!" he would beg me, grabbing my wrist that held a frog or some animal.

I would give in eventually. We slept in cold, dark nights under starry and starless skies and trudged on throughout the day. I had accepted in the third month that we were going to die. Finally, Jake and I began to eat berries and things that we found.

One day while we were foraging, he was too quiet for me. I knew that he had been extremely weak that day. Our regular sequence of operations was to whistle when the other found something in a certain pitch and to let the other know where we were. I found a patch of berries that we had eaten before. I was so excited that I did my whistle and began to eat. I don't know how long I had gone without hearing from him. I did my whistle again and waited...

No answer.

I knew what area he had been in and began to walk in that direction. I whistled every two to three seconds and still no answer. I began searching for him frantically. I did not call out for fear of being heard; I don't know by what. As I whistled and walked, I still heard nothing until finally I heard him moaning a few feet away from me. I ran to him and he was foaming at the mouth and shaking. His eyes were rolled into the back of his head. I looked at the patch nearby, and it was as though he wasn't thinking and began eating whatever. I found my vocal chords.

"JAKE!!! C'MON, MATE!! NO TOIME FA SLEEP, BUCKO!!" I screamed at him, slapping his face as I did at the orphanage. I heard rustling from somewhere near me, but I didn't care. Whatever was coming to get me would get us both. All the same, I reached for my dented and dulled knife. I was enraged that this was the moment for something or someone to find us. I was weak and delirious, Jake lay there dying, and I could do nothing about it.

I found out where the rustling was coming from and crouched down over his body with my back to the bush that he was sickened from. The rustling was getting louder. I tensed my muscles and bared my teeth. I can't remember if I was growling or not. I was told that I was. I tried to shush Jake, and the closer I crouched over his body, the warmer I felt him getting. The brush in front of me finally broke, and the man I saw before me was no threat- but I thought Applegum wasn't either, remember. He had an old rifle with him and he wore a red and black plaid shirt. His face was that of a saint and he instantly put the rifle down.

"Well, well, what do we have here?" the kind-faced man with grey hair said.

I just looked at him as menacing as I could. I held the knife out and had my feet by Jake's shoulders. I tried to cover his whole body with mine.

"Listen, Son, I don't have a weapon and I don't think you should have one either. I don't know what you have goin' on here but I don't think your friend looks too good. Give me a chance and I'll help," he said, crouching down eye to eye with me.

I held fast for a few seconds and looked him over to see if he had any other weapons on him. He reached out to touch the hand that I held the knife in, and I was too weak to strike out at him.

"Just put down what you have and I will do what I can. I am assuming that he had a go at those berries over there and that isn't good, but I can still do something now before they set in on him." He touched my hand

and it was warm. I dropped the knife and I don't remember if it was from him touching me or from weariness.

"Me brova, Jake. 'Es dyin', 'e is," I said weakly.

"Ahh! He speaks. No, your friend isn't dying at all, mate. He's just a little sick. Give me two of those leaves from that bush right there; we'll have him calmed in a jiffy," he said.

I grabbed two of the leaves and he asked for two more. With care, the man turned Jake onto his side and asked me to hold his mouth open and pull his tongue out. He rubbed the leaves on Jake's tongue vigorously.

"Just give him a few and he'll be fine," the man said. "What's your name, kiddo? Mine's Thomas. Thomas Wilschire," he said, extending his hand for me to shake.

I flinched and repositioned myself on top of Jake. I stared at him with no words.

"A shy one, are you? No problem. You two out here about your own wits, are you? Look at him, there he goes," Thomas said, looking at Jake.

I looked down and Jake was vomiting quietly. He had nothing on his stomach so it was mainly foam and berries. He went back to moaning and within minutes, he was asleep.

"Just let him rest here for a little while and you two will be fine to be on your way," Thomas said, sitting on the ground.

At that moment, I saw that he had a bag of what I assumed was food on his shoulder. Now, Thomas was a large man and he looked as though he could handle himself, but with the hunger I had, combined with the need of food for Jake, I cared not in the least. I snatched the knife from the ground, jumped over my sleeping brother and placed the dull knife against his throat.

"What is this, young one? I don't have anything of value. If I would have known this was a set up, I would have kept walking," he said, quickly raising his hands off the wet grass.

"Not tryin ta hurt ya, but…" I said, looking at the bag.

"It's just a sandwich my wife prepared for me. Take it if you'd like; it's plenty for you and your little friend here," he said.

"Brova. 'E's me brova," I replied as sharply as I could while grabbing his sack.

I dropped the knife again and tore into the satchel, biting one large hunk off the sandwich. I crouched back to Jake with him behind me and Thomas in front of me. He relaxed quickly for someone who had just had a knife to his neck—then I realized I had left the knife closer to him than to me as I was gobbling down another hunk of the food. I slowed my chews and looked back down at the knife. He looked at me and what he said shocked me.

"You need me to sharpen this for you?" He picked up the knife and handed it back to me.

I slowly took it from his hand. I was about to go back in for another bite and looked over my shoulder at Jake. I had to save him most of it. I wrapped up what was left and tears began to form in my eyes.

"Listen kiddo, my wife and I have plenty of food and shelter. If you want, you are welcome to come with me, clean up, and wait for your brother to heal up there," he said.

I knew at that point that I had no choice. I was defeated. My stomach growled again and I looked back down at the sandwich in my hand, then to Jake.

"It's not that hard of a choice to make, mate. You and ya brother don't look to make it too much longer out here," he explained.

"Troy," I said, laying my free hand on Jake's chest. His breathing was settled now.

"Pardon me, Son?" he asked.

"Me name's Troy," I said through tears.

"Well, no harm no foul, Troy. You may as well finish the sandwich yourself; he may be out for a while." I looked afriad. "Oh no, no, Troy, Jake will be fine, he just needs some rest while the antidote takes full effect. Now if you want, you can grab some more of the leaves and when he wakes he'll have a few before he tries and puts something on his stomach," he said reassuringly.

I picked a few more leaves from the bush near Jake. I did not want anyone but Jake to be in my life right then. In the situation that I was in, I trusted no one but him. Thomas stood up and picked up his rifle.

"Well, glad that's all settled now, right?" he said, extending his hand out again. For some reason, I still did not want to shake it- I can only assume it was fear of the unknown.

He shrugged his shoulders, went to pick up Jake, and I hissed at him. I actually hissed at him. Here this man was trying to assist us with as much as he could, and all I could do was hiss at him. He flinched. He knew that I would need him soon anyway. I finished gobbling down the sandwich and lifted Jake up. I could barely walk three paces before I fell. Thomas instantly turned to us. I fell on top of Jake and could only lay there. He picked Jake up like a bag of feathers and placed him on his shoulder opposite the rifle. He then came towards me and tried to pick me up.

"Me brova…help him," I struggled out.

"Understood, but everyone is not your enemy, Troy," he said, watching me struggle to get up.

Now, the food began to kick in and I was getting a small amount of energy back. But, I still was not strong enough to pick him back up and Thomas knew it.

"Help...Jake," I mustered out, standing up.

We walked for what seemed like hours, and we finally came upon a farmhouse. Thomas walked to the barn of the property, opened its doors, and turned to me with Jake slumped over his shoulder.

"I got a room inside for you both, but I can only bring Jake in when he feels up to snuff," he said.

It felt too suspicious to me and I pulled out my knife and stood defensively, baring my teeth and growling.

"Now, Troy, think before you get a bee in your bonnet. I'll set you in here if you want and I'll see what my wife says about you both staying inside," he said.

Thomas walked Jake inside, and I began to feel comfortable after watching him carefully place Jake on a bale of hay then setting up a nice bed for him and me. There were horses, cows and chickens all around. My mouth began to water. The tiredness of the previous weeks was weighing on my shoulders.

"Give me a sec there, bucko, and I'll let my wife know to get you something else to eat and see if we can find you somewhere to stay for a few nights," he said, leaving the barn.

What I found odd at that time was that the door was left open. I didn't trust it. I searched the entire inside of the barn, top to bottom, knife in hand. I did not want any threats coming from anywhere. After I was done, the tiredness came upon me with the weight of a whale. I crawled next to Jake with my tattered clothing and slid my knife into the hay beside me. I got behind my brother and hugged him close to my chest. He stirred a little and spoke to me, and it made me feel wonderful to hear his little voice.

"Troy...don't...eet...berries," he whispered quietly.

I hugged him tighter to me, he began to snore again, and I soon followed.

October 27, 1887

I stood there for three hours watching Yarney. He looked over his shoulder toward her house and walked off. I walked toward her front stoop and waited, watching him leave. I heard a tap at the upstairs room. I looked up and Tabitha was standing there. She was in the room where we shared many sexual encounters. And of course, Sarah was behind her. I was starting to think that Sarah likes Tabitha, and this made me smile. Tabitha didn't return the smile- she just beaconed me to come upstairs. I shook my head, "No." I looked back down the road and saw my target.

I had to think. Had she been in the house the whole time they were scouting around, and what is her plan? I needed to learn more about that woman in red. I followed Yarney about three blocks up the busy road during the darkening evening. He walked into the nearest tavern. I waited about thirty minutes and then walked in. I did my normal scan of the hostelry, and within seconds, I saw him bringing the well-dressed woman drinks near the end of the bar. As I continued my investigation, I knew she was in charge. She actually stabbed another of her lackeys in his hand and laughed while everyone else followed. I walked to the main serving table and continued to watch The Red Woman and Yarney.

"What are ya 'avin, luv?" the bartender asked with a smile.

Breaking my concentration almost sent me into a rage, and I wanted to slam one of the beer mugs into her teeth. I cleared my throat and calmly replied, "Yes, I'll have an ale and whiskey."

She walked off and brought my drinks. I turned back to the tavern's outer area. I couldn't really stare at them or even gain too much information from what I saw then. I stayed for an hour. In that hour, I did notice that the Red Woman was into men and women. I know that makes me want her dead. She thinks that she is in charge. She reminds me of Ms. Applegum, and that is enough. I abhor the Red Woman. I need to find a way to erase her.

I had not prepared for any artwork tonight, I thought to myself, placing my hands into my empty pockets. I was angry. What hadn't Tabitha told me? What was she hiding? I walked up the few blocks and popped over Tabitha's back fence. She stood on the back porch smoking a fag.

"Foind out all ya need about me loife, didja?" she asked, flicking the rest of her cigarette.

"I never knew you smoked. I detest that activity. My mother smoked," I said angrily.

We were both upset. I could tell she wanted to hit me by the way she stormed over to me. She was smarter than that though. She turned away from me, swearing, until finally:

"You 'ave no roight. Snoopin' in ta me loife loike 'at. She murdered the Queen's English.

"Well, you have no right hiding your interactions with thugs from me either. What were you, some sort of whore?" I asked, stepping through her garden.

I was still careful not to crumple anything. I was too close to her, for she turned and struck me. The rage began to bubble over like a top on a boiling pot of potatoes ready to be mashed. I could not wait to feel them squashed under my fists. All I could think about was how I wanted to drag her into the kitchen quietly and cut that infernal eye from its socket, until I saw her crying, and she said:

"'Ow dare ya stand there und judge me, Thomas?" She squinted her eyes.

Killing her would solve nothing. I wanted to know more about the Red Woman.

"I want ya gone, Thomas. Ya think I loike the way ya treat me? Ya stay gone fa 'ours. Ya have nay a feeling in ya bones. Ya fok loike a king, I mean I haven't had sex loike this in ever. But 'at's not oll I need. A big willy and great moves don't make the world, Thomas," she said, beginning to sob.

Sarah floated around her, laughing. She wanted Tabitha right then.

"See, ya just zone out sometoimes. I don't know what that is." She turned to walk in the house.

I grabbed her wrist. Sarah got pissed.

"Wait..." I said. "Who was Baggins? Why did he want to kill you? What happened to your eye?" I asked.

She stopped, held her head down, and then turned back to me, much calmer. She pulled her wrist from my hand gently.

"Foine. As soon as ya tell me yore story," she said, folding her arms in a winning stance.

I put my head down. I walked past her, got a glass, and poured myself an ale from the icebox. I then came back on the porch and stood in the shadows, looking at her in the moonlight. I told her everything. Of course not everything. I couldn't tell her about the murders the exact way they happened. Every time I told a lie, I made sure to look away from her eye. I told her that the black man killed my mother, about the orphanage, and that Jake and I had been adopted by the Wilschire's before it was burned down. I told her about my brother, Jake. I laughed to tears telling her about him. I told her about the abuse. Physical and emotional from my mother and sexual from Jerimiah at Happy Sunshine.

She pushed me against the wall, dropped to her knees, and orally satisfied me right there. She rinsed her mouth in her kitchen sink. When she came back in, she took my ale and drank a big gulp. She belched.

"So ya wan'a hear me background, eh?" She then began the story that changed the way I look at her.

Tabitha's Story

Tabitha told me she was in a military family. Her father was from India and her mother was from London. Her life wasn't as catastrophic as mine, but it was on the same path. London seems to always take a positive family structure and ruin it. Her mother had an older son from a previous marriage. Tabitha said she loved her brother more than life itself. He was one of the last men other than her dad to be kind to her. Tragically, they both died in a train yard accident.

One day when she came home from school, her mother was missing. At twelve she was too old to go to an orphanage, so she began working in taverns cleaning and serving the tenants of the hostelry. After she was raped at sixteen, she began carrying knives with her everywhere. She met up with Baggins and Rose two years later. They were a brother and sister team who were trying to make a name for themselves as a tough new gang. They were selling alcohol, cigarettes and women. And, since she had no alcohol or fags, she put herself on the market as the latter. I wanted to scream, hearing this from the woman I cared about. I could have slit her throat right then and there. But, I allowed her to continue. She said that, at first, Baggins had taken a liking to her, but that had been overshadowed by Rose's affections. She said that Rose had actually courted her, whereas Baggins just took her. She felt Rose had bought her. Tabitha even went as far as saying that I reminded her of Rose, emotionally that is. The reason is that I only abuse her in the bedroom, she said, patting my crotch with a smirk. If she only knew how fraudulent my laugh and smile had been. She went to light another cigarette and I smacked it from her hand.

"Oi,' 'at was me last one!" she exclaimed.

I have noticed that she speaks improperly when she's angry or aroused and I have grown accustomed to it. I now know why she has been so great in bed. I also understand why she is so upset that I followed the man Yarney today. She said that while her and Rose dated, she drank so much and took so many drugs that she looked into the mirror and hated how she looked. Tabitha has a body built like the latest steam engine. It runs perfectly. She was almost created for sex, every part of her is immaculate, even down to where each freckle lands on her. Some nights, I lay in bed next to her and caress her smooth, naked body. I cannot picture it any other way.

"At was the straw 'at broke the mule's back fa me," she said. "I packed me things at that moment. I 'ad to leave."

She said that after she packed all she could, she took one thousand dollars from Rose's personal purse.

"I didn't get far, for she caught me at the carriage, her n' Baggins. They took me ta a secluded area and took turns rapin' me," she said, taking another swig of my drink. I thought about not believing her, or shouting at her that she was a whore and that she got what she deserved. But I was torn between this. I listened anyway.

"Afta they had their go at me, ole Rosie pulled a noice lil hand blade and did this to me eye," she said, pointing to the left side of her face.

She began to sob. For the first time since she and I began seeing each other, I pulled her to me and hugged her.

"She said that eventually I'll keep seein' this blasted cut as her and come back to her," she said through her sobs.

I knew then that Rose was going to die. I want to kill her because, through all this, Tabitha loves her still. She hasn't said so, but I know. I can tell the way she was describing Rose and how she treated Tabitha in the beginning. Tabitha also needs to pay for becoming one of Them. I will pick this rose from her garden. I just need to clip her thorns.

November 2, 1887

My research had to begin on Rose fast, so I started last Monday. I needed to know all I could about her. Being a garbage man makes it easy to be in areas and not really be seen. All I did was take others' routes who did not want to work. I would only ask for a small portion of their pay that wouldn't hurt their pockets. They obliged me with no problem.

I stayed within a three-mile radius of where they were in the tavern. I saw her on a couple of days, but ended up losing her carriage with my slow horse. It was becoming very aggravating. I stopped seeing Tabitha for a while. My focus, stamina, and energy were on finding a pattern. Just something I could simply follow. On Thursday of that week, I was slowly collecting the garbage barrel to hopefully see something, when I saw Yarney and someone who I assume was the carriage driver.

"...Eight o' clock go' it? Rose will be comin' outta that alley at eight o' clock. 'Ow 'ard is this? It 'appens every Fursday. 'Ave the carriage there at that tiome, ya dolt," I overheard him saying while giving the guy a smack on the head.

I was overwhelmed with joy.

"This one will need preparation," I thought to myself.

Sarah and I smiled as I walked into the dark shadow of the underway leading to the next street.

I quickly made it home and checked my time. It was five forty p.m. I need to be out there by at the very least six twenty. If this happens every Thursday, as good ole Yarney says, then I will wait for the chloroform. I smile at the site of the little bottle. It reminds me of better times when I never thought this way.

March 3, 1866

That following morning, Jake and I awoke to the doors of the barn creaking open. I grabbed my knife on instinct, but it was too bright. I heard Jake snarl and the shuffling of hay to my lower right. He turned his little body to my rear and grabbed my ankle with his little hands. I taught him everything but the snarl. He knew I was going to protect him tooth and nail. Everything was just too damn white. I began to see a silhouette of a slender woman come into vision. I then heard the last angelic voice that I ever heard again.

"Oh my! Aren't you two just the cutest little buttons?" the voice said. "Thomas told me all about you two. Well, don't just stand there. C'mon, I made a breakfast to feed a whole town in there. My name's Betty Wilschire, by the way," she chirped.

She then disappeared into the whiteness. I tore my eyes away to look down for my brother. He was looking at me with pure terror in his eyes.

"Where 'r we, Troy?" he whispered, clearing his throat.

"Bloke saved ya. Ya were dun fore an' 'e 'eard me yellin' atcha ta get back on ya feet," I said.

"Me belly is still goin' on for sorts," he said.

That reminded me of what Thomas told me and I reached on top of the hay bale that Thomas left the leaves on. I motioned for him to stick out his tongue. I then rubbed the leaves as I saw Thomas do. Jake grimaced and winced, but only for a moment.

"Oi' did she say sumfin about food, mate? I am bloody stahvin!" he said, skipping to the door.

I tucked the dull knife into my tattered pocket and started behind Jake. We walked out, and Mrs. Wilschire was a beauty to behold. She had long brown hair with small streaks of grey forming patches here and there. She had honey brown eyes and a wonderful smile. Small but noticeable crow's feet were forming in the corners of her eyes, but they only added to her kind and wisdom-infused face. She wore the typical housedress and apron, which only made her more motherly.

"C'mon, C'mon, C'mon, wash up now- got plenty for you boys to eat," she said.

Jake crept over first and washed his hands and face very fast. I paused, gathered my surroundings, and followed. After we finished, she led us into the large, two story home with white windows. We walked into a kitchen, and the smells were so delightful that Jake stole a look at me. He had the largest smile I had ever seen on him. I was pleased, but nervous. In front of us was a large, round table with all sorts of different breakfast foods. Some of which I hadn't even heard of at that time. Thomas was sitting at the head of the table and Betty sat beside him. There were three more chairs at the table and Jake and I sat next to one another. We ate. Every bite was a symphony of marvelous. I had never known a food to have this effect on a person.

"Wow, hun, look at them go," she said to Thomas.

"Yeah, they seemed to be out there for some time, dear. Hey, by the way, where are you youngins from?" he asked.

Jake stopped chewing and looked up at me. He was terrified. I kept my head down and continued eating. Jake popped another piece of bacon in his mouth and nudged me under the table. I hissed at him. He knew this meant to keep eating.

"No sir, you will not go on the sorts like that to your friend—"Betty began.

"Brova, 'e's me brova. Orphanage," I quickly spat out.

I gave Thomas a cold stare for a moment. She was no threat; he was. For some reason, his face did not change. He was calm and very collected. I then went back to eating. Betty had a look of confusion on her face, then turned back to Thomas. He held his hand up to her and spoke back to me. He was still calm; I could tell it would take a lot to get any type of reaction from him. I didn't know how to deal with him. I would wait until he made his move. I could be just as calm.

"Troy, do you know the name of the place? I'm sure they are worried sick about you two," he said.

Jake had started his fidgeting thing again. He had even stopped eating. I could see him from the corner of my eye; every time one of us spoke, he would look at whoever was talking. I was becoming irritated and he knew it.

"They all doied. Foire," I said.

Betty covered her mouth.

"Oh my gracious!"

Thomas sat up in his seat. This was the first reaction that I saw from him. He was now focused on Jake, who had tears streaming from his eyes. Thomas was concerned for Jake.

"What's a' matter, boyo?" he asked Jake.

Before Jake could say a word, I answered for him.

"Heez foine," I said to Thomas. "Eet," I said to Jake without removing my eyes from Thomas.

"Hey, you both have an equal right to communicate. Don't do that to him again," Thomas said.

He directed his attention back to me and this time he had a stern look on his face. He had approached Jake to see if I would react the same way again. And I did. I learned that day that he was a lot smarter than I thought. This angered me even more. My rage was building due to a few things. I was mad at Jake for crying. The Wilschires' fucking questions were getting under my skin. But most of all, I was pissed at the Applegum's for putting Jake and I in this whole barrel. I slammed my hands on the table and erupted:

"YEAH, IT BURNED DOWN AND I 'OPE THEY BURNED WITH IT!" I screamed.

Jake was balling at this time and bolted for the door. I hissed and grunted at him to sit down. He didn't listen. He was gone outside. Betty's eyes were the size of eggs. Thomas had the same stone look on his face. There was no fear at home there. He looked the same way when I put the knife to his throat. He was ready. I hated how cool he was that day. In my mind, I was a monster and there was no one who could not be done for if they crossed me. But, Thomas was no more worried than if he had seen a rabbit eating a carrot in front of him.

"Betty," he said quietly.

She had her eyes fixed on me.

"Betty, hun?' he said in a sturdier tone.

"Y-Yes, dear?" she replied.

It was as if once she realized how calm he was, she instantly relaxed. He was the alpha male in this situation and I had not realized it before I exposed myself.

"Go see if you can find Jake and make sure he's done with the tears. Good ole Troy-boy and I are going to have a nice tête-à-tête," Thomas said.

"Oh, of course," she said.

"I'll let ya know when everything is on the up and up," he said.

She nodded and disappeared out the door.

"Now, Troy-boy, it's you and me. If ya feel the need to take out your anger on whatever ya have been through, then feel free. Do it on me. You got a free chance. You wanna use that dull knife of yours? If you don't have it with you, I'll let you get it. But one thing you won't do is scare Jake and my wife. Did that make you feel good? You like to make your brother cry? You seem to care about him somewhat. Is that what you think he likes to see from you?" he asked. He was too calm.

My heartbeat slowed and I could feel my breathing steadying. All I could see was how terrified Jake was of me when I took care of Jeremiah and his lovely mother. Thomas was skilled at calming the situation. He didn't live my horrors. He didn't know how many times Jake and I had to fight off animals and monsters in that wilderness. And I am not just talking about the forest. But it didn't feel good making Jake cry. I didn't care about Betty at that time; I was upset that Jake was gone. I couldn't blame him though, he was nine. He didn't want to even see what he witnessed at that orphanage and it was my fault. The forest was actually easier for me than my own life. Thomas watched me think about the words that I didn't understand. He held his hand out for me to sit back down. I pulled out my knife. His hand did not move.

"What you can do is sit back down and finish your breakfast. We will sit here like civilized humans and converse. I promise you that that knife won't be needed as long as you are on this farm," he said.

I began to sit down and tears were forming in my eyes. I placed the knife on the table and was about to take my hand off when I heard Jake scream. I instantly lost any sorrow I was feeling and bolted to the door.

"TROY!! HE'S MINE!!" I heard Thomas say.

I knew it was all a ploy for us to let our guard down. Why did they want him? When I got outside, I whistled for Jake, and I heard his scream again and ran in that direction. I could hear Thomas behind me moving chairs out of his way. I was still smart enough to be closer to the door than he was at least. Jake screamed again and my feet were moving too slow. I ran to the back of the barn and saw Mrs. Wilschire on the ground with her back to me. All I saw was Jake's little black legs hanging off her lap and the top of his little, black, sheep's fur head. What was she doing to him? I had no clue what they were planning to do to him. I had to free my brother, so I raised my knife. I knew it was dull, but it would be sharp enough to do this job. I could hear Thomas' feet closing in on me and I had to act fast. Then Jake screamed again, but this time with laughter. I froze.

"TROY- HE'S FINE I SAID!"

Betty turned her head. Upon seeing me, she squeezed Jake and held him to her chest as tight as she could. I fell to my knees and fainted. Everything broke.

When I woke up, Thomas explained that this was too much for me to take. I was in the bedroom of his son who had died in the war. Thomas said he would explain all that to me in time.

"Here's your knife, Troy-boy," he said, handing me my knife.

I moved it and his hand from in front of my face, slowly.

"Jake?" I asked.

"He's outside. He was worried about you but we talked him down. You boys have been through a lot and we can tell. I will tell you the same thing that I told Jake. You two can stay here as long as you need. We could use the help and company here. But, I will tell you something, Troy-boy. If you don't want to stay, Jake has already said he wanted to. I won't let you scare him into leaving with you."

I knew that he would have made sure of it. If I was to leave and Jake wanted to stay, then I wouldn't have made him leave with me. Thomas could see that. He placed the knife on the dresser next to the bed, got up, and walked from the room. Soon, I saw my little brother's head bobbing in. The bed was very tall and comfortable. If we stayed here, he would have this bed.

"Troy? What's got in ta ya, mate?" he asked meekly. "Dey din't 'urt ya, mate. 'At was Jeremiah an''at witch. Kent take it out on 'em. I can't be 'ere if ya gonna be doin' what ya did ta Applegum and 'er seed," he said.

I shook my head "no" to him and held my arms out for a hug. He climbed his little body up in the bed and hugged me.

"Ya promised me ya wouldn't do 'at again," he said, laying on my chest.

Jake didn't know how much I was trying to keep my promise.

Over the next month or two, I learned that Thomas was a taxidermist. I had no clue what that was at the time. He introduced me to chloroform and what it did to small animals.

"Now, Troy-boy," (that became my new nickname for some reason) "don't you and Jake start playing with this sort of stuff, because you may not wake up, or worse, lose an arm," he said.

I didn't realize that he was exaggerating until later in life. But then, my eyes became huge as I watched a squirrel struggle with the chemical. I snickered as he fell into a peaceful slumber. Thomas then showed me how to gut the animal and the importance of doing so. Hmm. Jake was right after all.

November 22, 1887

I arrived around six forty five based on my pocket watch. It was the third Thursday, and I waited until eight o' clock. I knew it was smart to wait until I was sure. All three nights she was on time. So now, I have a week to get to her. After work last week, I tested the chloroform on myself. I wanted to know how long its potency would last. That Friday evening through Monday, I did not leave my room. I poured a very small amount on a rag and let it sit for at least three hours before getting a good whiff.

Now, seeing its effects on a small squirrel from a cotton ball amount was one thing. But a five foot seven, one hundred forty five pound woman in a back alley while she struggles is a different story all together. So, I will take the risk. After the three-hour experiment, I then tried different times. I was able to obtain an ample amount of the chemical because doctors don't really like to use it much. I would hold the rag to my face to feel its effects. After I felt the wooziness, I was comfortable.

I can soak my gloves with the substance since they are leather, but I will need some type of protection against the dangerous chemical. I will wrap one of my hands with gauze, but that hand will have two jobs. I will need to hold the rag to her face and restrain her while she struggles. The other hand will need to make the proper cuts. I've decided to use my right hand to hold her and cut the glove so it will fit over the gauze wrapped hand. As I worked my routes today, I thought about how it will feel to use my knife again on Their flesh. I was so excited that I actually carried the knife to work that I had sharpened throughout the previous night. I would carefully reach into my pocket every so often to touch the blade.

"Thomas!" I heard Tabitha shout.

That was exactly what wasn't needed right now. I needed to keep my mind clear. I turned to her, trying to collect my thoughts. The only problem I had was lying to that eye of hers.

"Yes, hello Tabitha," I said.

"So that's oll I'm worth now?" she asked.

"Oh no, my dear. I was just focused on my job here," I made up. "How have you been?" I asked.

"Foine.' Aven't seen ya in a while. Did I offend ya?" she asked.

"Oh no, I've just been working a lot of different hours," I stated.

She looked at me. Then the eye looked at—no through-- me. It knew I was up to something. I think it even knows and actually sees Sarah. I even think that Tabitha knows but is too afraid to tell me. She may not even believe what she is seeing, so in her mind she may feel it is best to keep silent.

"So now ya woikin' oll day 'n night now, guvna? Mm. And when will I be able ta see ya and our friend down thea?" she asked with a smirk.

"Well actually, I have the day off next Thursday and we will be able to spend it together- worry-free," I said.

After what will be done then, Tabitha and I will be worry-free. But, the eye. That eye can tell. It knows that it will always be us three. I cannot lie to the grey marble in Tabitha's head about Sarah.

"'Ats all foine and dandy Thomas. I just want it to be you and me. Why can't we just be alone? Whoever else it is, I don't loike bein second ta any otha whore on this planet," she stated.

Sarah and I almost both laughed, but I silenced myself. Her left eye almost seemed to blink.

"Trust me, my dear…" I said, stroking her cheek, "…there is no woman on this planet second to you."

The eye was satisfied. I smiled. I know now that eye has it out for me. This time I had it in checkmate.

"Okay sweets, I'll be looking forward to it," she said, rubbing her firm bottom on my crotch.

She turned and gave me a small smooch on my cheek and walked off. We were at the market. She had eggs and meats. Sexually, I wanted her, but I didn't want her to like it. As she disappeared into the crowd, I looked over across the road and in between the flowing carriages and bustling people, I looked into the alley of our next victim. Sarah, in her black, lacey, wet-looking evening gown was there with her dark grey, scaly skin. She spinned in the darkness and beaconed me into the shadows.

November 29, 1887

Today, I was eager to finish my route. I wanted to head back out after work to see what was down that alley. I finished my day's work early and rushed home. I got dressed in the most normal and unnoticeable outfit that I have. I wanted to learn as much as I could about the hidden areas so that I could lay in wait for her.

There was a popcorn trolley. I bought a bag and walked up the opposite side of the street of the alley. It was about twelve noon, and the shadows were ever darkening. I walked across the road and confidently went into the dark corridor. The alley was in between two buildings, one shorter than the other. But there was only one exit to the alley with the two buildings on the side. One was apparently an apartment. There were a couple of quick areas that I could possibly conceal myself in.

Out of a shadow from the corner of my eye, I saw a small movement. I shifted my focus. It was a little difficult to focus on the movement due to the steam from various pipes, but there was some type of black blanket on the ground just out of the sunlight's reach. I looked around and no one was there but me. The blanket was moving rhythmically up and down as though there were two mice moving underneath, but every time it went up, whatever was underneath seemed to be getting larger. It went from the size of mice to a small dog and then to a baby bear cub.

I could then hear a painful moaning in my head. I knew it had to be inside because there was no echo in the sound. For some reason, my feet were compelled to continue towards this thing. I felt the beads of sweat under my hat forming. I licked my lips and wanted to say something, but no words formed. My testicles tightened in my lower regions. I could not be dreaming because everything was too real. I stopped when I heard the familiar scream. The blanket had then grown to the size of a human and it was now forming the lacey black dress that Sarah always wears now. Her hands came from the sleeves and they were just barely covered in any skin. She hissed as her head came from the top of the dress.

I was close enough then for either of us to reach out and touch. But, she floated closer to me still. The smell was almost unbearable. She was close enough to me now as if she wanted to kiss me. Her eyes were solid white and her skin was almost thin enough to be transparent. Maggots, worms and other bugs had made a home in her face. When she spoke, her black tongue had even more black bugs skittering from under it. Her teeth were jagged and decayed with sharp, pointy ends. Parts of her lips were missing where various things and mildew had eaten away at them.

"Let me show you, my sweet," she whispered, touching my face.

Her hands felt like a cold, slimy mist against my warm skin. She leaned her face toward mine and opened her mouth. I was in so much fear, I didn't think to close mine. I felt her tongue investigating mine. The taste made me squint and tears flowed from my eyes. When I reopened them, I was in a darker version of the alleyway I was in. I turned around, and Rose was walking directly towards me. In my shock, I reached for my knife and swiped at her throat, but it went through her. This was a vision. Sarah was nowhere in view and this was what she wanted me to see. Rose walked through me the same way my knife went through her. I wiped my tears and followed. As I walked, areas that were very shadowed turned bright. Sarah was showing me where I could hide tonight. I smiled.

The mist cleared, yet I was still standing where she appeared in front of me. My jaw felt as though it was locked into the open position for too long. It popped when I finally closed it. I felt drained and weak. When I looked back to where the black blanket was, there was nothing but trash. I fell to my knees and vomited all the popcorn on the ground. I wiped my face and stared where she had appeared. I stood and turned away, realizing what I needed to do. I walked to the entrance and looked around. I headed home.

This is going to be difficult because there will be people out and about. Adding to that, there is no rear exit to that alley. I will worry about that when it arrives. I'm beginning to get things together. I always use multiple weapons. But tonight, I won't take as many since I will be killing her before the carriage arrives. I won't have time to really cut any off her, but the chloroform will take a lot of the fight out of her. I'm laughing out loud this time, looking at the little bottle.

August 03, 1867

I learned how to read and write from the Wilschire's. They treated Jake and me as their own. We were happy to work on that farm. We would chop wood in the winter and collect the harvest in the summer. We became stronger. I mean, we had no choice. I had never cut wood before or worked in a garden. I remember when Jake first worked in the garden, for the first complete week he almost cried every day when he woke up due to the soreness. I had a couple of tears in my eyes the first day, but I couldn't show him. I needed him to see me as the strong one, but he was getting stronger every day.

The Wilschire's were a perfect match for the hell that we had come from. Mrs. Wilshire cooked amazing meals while Thomas taught us life lessons. Things like hunting, fighting, and chess. Jake had grown to almost my height within the first year we were there. Within that time, I had begun to trust them alone with Jake. Now that I look back, I feel so stupid for the choosing to be violent towards them. I was the problem and Thomas had shown me that. I almost didn't like racing or wrestling Jake because he had gotten so fast and strong so quickly, but we were the best of brothers. I was so proud of him when he killed his first deer and didn't cry. He and Thomas came home with his kill. He bustled in the door with a large smile on his face.

"Look Ma, I keeled it and I won't even cryin'!" Jake exclaimed.

He carefully placed the rifle on the ground by the stove. He then ran over to Betty, giving her a huge hug. She laughed, leaned down, and kissed him all over his little brown face.

"Oh my, look at my strong man. But it's 'killed' and 'wasn't', and there is a 'g' at the end of crying, Sonny. Now try again," she said.

I snickered while peeling potatoes at the huge dinner table. She held her hand up to me and I instantly stopped. Jake was very frustrated with his English. He rolled his eyes and huffed. Mrs. Wilschire explained to us countless times that she hated improper English, so she worked with us daily to make sure we didn't forget. Jake began again and she mouthed the words with him.

"Ma, I killed it--," he began.

"Killed what, dear?" she asked.

"Ma, I killed the deer and I wasn't even crying," he said.

At that time, Thomas came in.

"I am so proud of you, my little baby," she said, kissing him again.

She was aware that she had to baby Jake and not me so much. I didn't mind because Thomas made up for it by keeping me into the macho stuff. I will admit that they made a perfect team. He went over and kissed Betty.

"He tell you?" He asked her.

"Yes, hon. Sonny, go wash up and get ready for dinner. And when you come back down, help your brother with these potatoes. He looks like he needs it." She looked at me and smiled.

Thomas came over and ruffled my black, short cut hair. Thomas didn't have trouble cutting my hair, but when it came to Jake he would have a little trouble. He would do the best he could. Jake was always happy with it.

"Ya wanna see ya little brother's haul?" he asked.

The potatoes brought up many memories, so I jumped out of my seat and headed for the door.

"Thomas Wilschire!" Betty exclaimed.

"He'll only be a second, hon," he responded.

"Yeah. We'll be right back, Mrs. B.," I said

It had only been a year and I couldn't be as comfortable as Jake was. She was better than my mother ever was, but I still kept saying 'Mrs. B'. She was never bothered by it.

"Yes, Troy-boy, but I still need those potatoes for mash," she said.

Jake ran down and sat in front of the large pot of potatoes. Jake was always right on time from day one. Thomas and I seized the opportunity and ran out of the house.

"What?" I heard Jake ask Betty as we closed the door.

Thomas laughed. It took me months before I was able to stomach the sight of mashed potatoes and I would never eat steak again. The bothersome thing was that Jake loved mashed potatoes. Even years later, my insides would squirm when I was served potatoes. The first time I was given steak and potatoes, I cried and went upstairs to our room. Betty finally had to bring me a sandwich and milk. Thomas squatted down and looked up at me.

"Ya ready?" he asked.

I nodded. I felt something in my chest when he reached down to the tarp where the hooves were hanging out. I thought it was fear initially, but I know now it was pride. I was proud of Jake and wanted to see what he had accomplished. When he pulled the tarp back, I saw Jeremiah's head on the deer with a large bullet hole in the center of his skull. His fat, pulsing lips peeled back to show his grayish brown teeth. Blood bubbled from between the spaces of his teeth and his mouth as he smiled up at me.

"See, muffin? Ya litlo bruva's jost as much a killa as yoo 'r. Killed me reel good, 'e did." His voice was warped and sounded like he and his mother's together.

I wanted to claw my eyes out to not see it anymore. I wanted to scream. I wanted to run away. I looked down at Thomas. He instantly lost his proud smile when he saw my face and became concerned. I glanced back down at the deer and it looked normal.

"What's on ya, Troy-boy?" Thomas asked.

I couldn't tell him what I saw. My facial expression must have been one of complete terror. His words were trembling.

"Oi! Kiddo, ya pissing ya self!" Thomas exclaimed.

At this point, what does a thirteen-year-old boy who has killed many rabbits and deer of his own say to this? I tried to fake a smile.

"I'm just so happy for Jake," I said.

I ran into the house and up to the washroom to clean myself off. That night, Jake and I lay in our beds. We could have our own rooms with separate beds, but neither of us wanted to sleep that far from each other. The Wilschire's had to settle for separate beds.

"What 'appened when Pee-Pa showed ya me deer?" he asked.

I shivered in between my covers. All I could see was Jeremiah's head on top of the deer, smiling at me through bloody teeth.

"Nothin'. Why?" I replied.

I turned over in my bed. We talked however we wanted when we were alone. Jake had never known his father and his mother- they died at an early age. So, for the last year, he looked at the Wilschire's as his parents.

"Pee-Pa said sumfin' scared ya reel bad. Did my deer make ya sad or sumfin'?" he asked

I sat up in the bed and looked over at him in the darkness. I could see his little nappy head and forehead.

"No Jake, no. I was so happy I couldn't contain meself," I lied.

I hated lying to him, but I didn't want him to remember anything about that god forsaken orphanage. He knew about my nightmares. The days that I woke up with him in my bed was because he heard how bad the dreams were. He told me one morning that he felt he needed to hug me. And when he did, I would quiet down and sleep soundly. We had two more years of peace at the Wilschire's. Two years before I broke my promise to Jake to not commit murder.

November 29, 1887

After a good soaking of the glove, I wrapped my right hand in a gauze bandage, carefully making sure that my fingertips were completely covered. Checking my pocket watch, I had about two hours. I worked my way out of my back window. I was excited when I left my alley unseen, but the closer I got to my visual point from across from the area of attack, I began to feel anxious. As if I shouldn't have been there.

Sarah appeared before me to make me feel at peace. She made me feel that the artwork I was about to perform tonight would be warranted. I was beginning to want this to be over. I thought about Tabitha. Maybe I could be nicer to her. We could have what the Wilschire's had. Well, that is until they died.

I had to walk around to seem as if I was just admiring the scenery. There were almost too many people around. I could not really concentrate. It was as though something was hindering me from focusing. All I could think about was cutting Rose to pieces and what it would feel like. I was still able to keep myself as nonchalant as possible. I wanted to make sure I went in right before the carriage pulled up.

I walked up the main road around the alley until seven forty five. I headed right to the alley. There appeared to be less people now, so I was unseen. I assumed people were either in taverns or at home. I had enough time to duck into the alley before I heard the familiar click-clack of the horse's hooves. All the hidden places meant nothing at this point, because just like in the vision, Rose was coming directly towards me. Luckily, I already had my hands in my pockets. As we got close enough to pass one another, I can only assume she saw my face and realized my intentions. She knew why I was there. She began to reach under her overcoat for the silver one-shot pistol but I was too close. My knife went into her chest and its blade was long enough to puncture her ribcage. My left hand went to her wrist as she grabbed for the butt of the gun. I released my knife, still in her, and put my right hand over her nose and mouth.

"You prickly lilto willy..." she got out before I covered her mouth.

She tried to take in a deep breath when the blade penetrated her lung, but the air leaked out in a satisfying gush. The only problem was that the chloroform would take some time now. I was stronger than she was and had the surprise advantage. Sarah was in my head. Her, my heart rate, and my breathing canceled any outside noise. I pushed her against the wall to knock more wind from her now crippled lungs. With her free hand, she reached for the knife. I could see and feel the chloroform taking effect. Her gun hand began to drift away and her legs began to go. She began to realize her fate; I saw that her eyes had tears flowing from them. Sarah wanted to lick them from her whore face. Her hand finally released from the butt of the pistol.

"Take the pistol, my love," Sarah whispered in my ear, or in my brain. At that point, I was too excited to know. Her words felt like a misty kiss on my mind.

Rose finally began to go limp at that time, and I could not reach the weapon, for I was trying not to make a sound. I helped her to the ground, sliding the knife from her ribcage. The blood began to flow from her wound as a faucet. I just needed to do one thing before she fully passed out. I tried to carefully slice her from cheek to forehead over the same eye as Tabitha's. The only thing was that in all my excitement, I got too deep and cut through the eye, slicing it's milky center. The eye fluid mixed with her tears and blood and made a cloudy maroon dribble down her cheek. Sarah loved it, and Rose shuddered.

"...Uhhh..." she wheezed.

There was a slight whistling sound coming from her chest cavity. I was squatting over my artwork in progress when suddenly someone grabbed my shoulder. I was instantly enraged. My artwork has become very important to me, and for someone to interrupt, I found renewed energy to paint more.

"They must pay!" Sarah and I said.

When I stood and turned, I struck at the first thing I saw. Or, what Sarah allowed me to see. That damned grey eye. That little bloody tale-tell cloudy marble. It will never know when or if I am lying again. At this point, I realized we were speaking aloud.

"We are invisible to you all. You all will only see our artwork. We will never be seen," we whispered as my knife found its target with proficiency. As it sliced through the eye and went into the socket, I felt the bone around it split. The splitting effect made the rest of the blade slice through the rest of her skull easily. She made a choking sound as she fell backward.

"Behind you, my love," Sarah again whispered to me.

When I turned back, Rose had turned herself over and had her gun trained on me. She was lying on her belly now, looking at me with her good eye. The sound alone would draw massive attention. As fast as possible, I shot toward her gun and pulled the barrel into my right shoulder before she pulled the trigger. I tried to get it out of her hand, but she squeezed and the pain made me wince. Sarah instantly touched my shoulder and her cold fingers eased the pain from the pistol shot immensely. My left hand acted on its own and interjected the knife into her throat. She could not gasp, so her body jumped as though she had death hiccups. Blood spurted from her throat, mouth and burst eye socket.

The pain in my shoulder was so far away that I laughed. I actually laughed, or maybe it was Sarah and I that both laughed. The gunshot wound began to make the killing haze leave my mind like cleaning cobwebs from an attic. I felt like I was coming out of a dream. I stood up and thought. Reaching into my inside pocket, I checked my watch and it was eight o' clock on the nose. I looked at the mouth of the alley way and there was no carriage there. He was late! Perfect. I wanted her to be seen with her eye split open. That would be my present to Tabitha. But wait, who was the other art piece?

I smiled as I walked toward the body shaking on the ground near Rose. But my smile began to fade. I recognized that housedress. I saw the scar on her face, freshly opened. It was TABITHA!! What was she doing here? NO! NO! NO! I fell back against a trash barrel and bit my fist. Tears were falling from my face in warm, salty streams. My legs felt like wet noodles. I fell to the ground, staring at her body as it lost the last of its life. Sarah's laugh made me jump. I looked over to Rose's facedown body, and there was an aura like the one around Baggins, and Sarah was floating over her in the same manner. She was hunched over while Rose's aura made Sarah's aura much brighter than her brother's did. I even saw her black hair change back to its living auburn color. Rose's body even seemed to be vibrating. And Sarah's laughter seemed to be more human than it had the past few times that I heard it. I began to feel woozy for some reason, and I realized I was biting the right glove with the chloroform on it. I snatched my hand away and looked back to Sarah. She looked at me and floated over to Tabitha.

"No!" I whispered loudly.

Sarah covered her now brightening mouth with her hand and laughed at me. She was looking less and less ghastly.

"No, please don't, not her," I whispered again.

Sarah's body quickly went back to its ghastly form with her black hair and dress and moldy, mildew-like skin. When she screamed at me, the wind took off my top hat. She smelled like the same putrid things that I have smelled in the past. Tabitha did not deserve this, but I was too dizzy to try and stop Sarah. She floated to the top of Tabitha's body and did the same to her. Her body was purer than the first. I looked away; I did not want this for Tabitha, but I had to complete my artwork. Since I did not bring a butcher's knife with me tonight, I would have a hard time getting what I needed from the pieces.

Then, I knew Sarah was blocking my senses. I could almost remember hearing Tabitha call my name as I was cutting Rose' face. Sarah had this all planned. My mind was losing its weariness. As she finished up with Tabitha, she looked at me, then at the exit of the alley. She was right. I needed to get out of there, but first I took hold of my knife once again and went to Tabitha and then Rose. I made my way to the exit. Then I heard the horses' hooves. I made it across the street and hid in the shadows of steps by a housing unit. The carriage pulled up and the lunk driving it checked his own pocket watch. I could tell he realized that he was late.

I watched because I wanted to see his expression when he got off that seat of his and saw what I created down that alley. It was a shame that he would have to see Tabitha the way I did not want her to be seen. Seeing his face would put my mind at rest about Tabitha and Sarah.

She just couldn't let me have her. I know that there was potential for Tabitha and me to be happy. Sarah could have been involved as well, but later. Tabitha would have understood. Sarah just did not want to give her a chance. Sarah used my paintings as a way to take Tabitha away from me. That's fine Sarah, that's fine. We will see who has the last laugh. Sarah floated in front of me with her youthful look now. No longer was she decayed or mildewed. The driver sat on top of the carriage and waited for a moment, then climbed down to go into the alley to look for Rose. He disappeared, just to run back from the alley with a look of horror on his face.

I smiled, but I was still not happy. Sarah was not bothered by my anger in the least. She will soon know what this feels like- to not have any friends as she would like. I did not love Tabitha, but the tears still will not stop running down my cheeks.

I watched as the lunk ran off, apparently to find the closest bobby he could. I got up and walked in the opposite direction. Sarah has really lost her scruples. I don't know what she wants now. I was under the assumption that she wanted our happiness, but I am seeing that it is just her happiness that's on the top of her list. As I walked down the now aroused streets, I wondered how Sarah was able to keep me from seeing Tabitha.

December 2, 1887

I've cried for three days while looking at the items I took from Tabitha and Rose. I had to put them in jars to keep them as fresh as possible. Today, I went to work. Since I go in before the actual paper on my route arrives, I visited the paper vendor. On the front page of today's paper, I saw a large article with a name that they are giving the 'murderer:'

Jack the Ripper has claimed two more victims!
When will his reign of terror cease?

Now that I saw this in big, bold lettering, I had to buy a paper. After getting around the corner from the vendor, I laughed until I was in tears. The article went on to explain that the "Ripper," as they call him, is going around and cutting women up in all sorts of vicious ways. They say that they're using the word 'Ripper' because the women looked as though they were ripped apart, or open. My laughter faded as I continued to read.

I am no longer amused, because not once did they say that these murders were works of art. I do not know how to take any of what I read. They even combined the other two murders with these last two. One of the investigators was quoted as saying that the murders looked like a ghost committed them. This made me smirk. The bobbies were saying that since the women were cut up the same way, that that is the connection, and they were completely baffled. The writer of the article in the paper seems to be upset that I took Tabitha's heart and Rose's right eye.

I don't find it amusing that they refer to 'Jack' as a monster. I've read the article at least three or four times throughout the day. I've been looking for any changes or anything that mention that the bodies were not killed, but cut in ways that made them perfect. I was aiming for perfection despite the fact that they thought I had *only* murdered these women. But Tabitha, my sweet Tabitha. She was not supposed to be one of the art pieces. I was thinking about changing how I felt about her. She would soon have been someone that I could clearly confide in. I waited too late to tell another person once before- and I wish I hadn't.

September 17, 1868

Thomas was the best instructor on all things, it seemed. He and I would play chess all hours of the night, with Jake sitting beside us watching or dozing off. He didn't always want to play, but when he did he would get frustrated. But not me. I would lose to Thomas millions of times, but I would continue to play him. I did not mind losing. There were times that he would have to stop playing because Betty would come to the door looking upset. She was actually happy; she told me that it made her feel as though her son was still alive. Chess was a game that had the potential to change a person's mind. I loved the game.

But at any rate, Thomas had a lot of land that he could hunt, fish, and just plain live off of. We would walk and talk for hours. Jake either would be behind us or running ahead of us somewhere. He was proud of his deer kill. Jake didn't mind not carrying a rifle; he just wanted Thomas, him and me together. If Betty had joined us, it would have been excitement overload. Jake had learned so much over the three years we were there. He had become an individual. He and I did not have the same personalities. I loved him and he loved me; we were inseparable. Thomas and Betty even recognized this.

"So what happened at the orphanage?" Thomas asked one day, washing his hands in a nearby creek.

I had no words. I didn't know what to say. Jake was far enough away to not really hear our conversation. I didn't hear one bird or cricket chirping at that time. It was completely quiet. But this time, with Thomas' questioning, I did not get angered. I felt no level of rage or anything from this question. I think Thomas knew it. He was great at keeping a person calm in an otherwise uneasy situation. I just leaned against a random tree and looked off into nothingness. I was hoping to see some type of game before I had to answer.

"Ya gotta talk to someone about your problems. Why not me?" he asked.

"Well, it wasn't a nice time, I can tell you that much," I said. "I met people who didn't have my best interests in mind, until I met Jake. I didn't trust nobody and he didn't either. But for some reason we ended up trusting each other," I further stated.

"Well, Betty and I were talking the other night and wanted to know about the fire," he said.

I was so glad that Jake was not around. I knew he would have been fidgeting his ass all over the place.

"The fire was sumfin that happened after we ran away. We didn't know anything about it till we saw it from a distance. We just wanted to get out of there," I lied.

Thomas knew it. When I looked back at him, his face was perplexed. I didn't know if my lying was something that he could tell or not. I was going to go with this anyway.

"Why couldn't you just tell us that in the beginning?" he asked. I could tell he did not believe me based upon that question.

I didn't know how to answer, so I just fell silent.

"Let's go, Troy-boy, I don't care too much about it anymore. The Missus, she has all the questions in the world. Let's go find--," he began, but the sound of a rifle stopped him.

"Jake!!!" we both screamed.

We ran towards the direction of the gunshot. I don't know if I heard Jake crying or the men talking first, but whatever it was, my knife was instantly in my hand. Somehow, I had dropped the rifle I was carrying. After the Applegum's, my knife was my favorite weapon of choice. I enjoyed cutting into the flesh of my enemies. As we got closer to Jake, Thomas put his hand on my chest and a finger to his lips. He motioned for me to go home and he knew I would say no. He then motioned for me to go around where we were hearing the voices and to wait for him. He removed his shoes and held them in his hand as a suggestion for me to do the same. I was used to not using words, so I understood all his gestures. This was my chance to make him proud and show him I didn't just kill game. He had actually bought me another knife after a while. He said that he never knew when something bad would happen and he wouldn't be around.

I crept on all fours with the knife in between my teeth. As I went around, I saw through the bushes that Jake was on his knees and covering his ears, with tears streaming down his face. I was upset at myself for allowing my little brother to get into this position. Thomas must have known that I wouldn't wait for him, but he acted anyway. There were four men around Jake and they were just terrorizing him, but I couldn't really understand what they were saying because they had some weird way of talking. At fifteen, I didn't realize they were Irish, until Thomas later told me. I got into a good position and whistled like a bird. Jake knew what it was and stopped crying instantly. He stood up and turned his back to my position like he was supposed to. Thomas crashed in and hit one of the men with the butt of his rifle, laying the man out. He then aimed at one of the other men. I repositioned myself to get behind him.

"Drop your gun right now, and don't make any moves!" Thomas said in a voice that I had never heard him use before.

I could tell he was angry because he was talking through bared teeth.

"Don't try and be a hero; just do what I tell you and you'll be fine. But you better do it now!" he yelled.

I could tell that one of the other two men was deciding on what to do, so I came from the bushes and snatched him back into the shrubbery to help make his decision for him. I was strong, but I did not realize how much my strength had grown. He didn't really try and put up a fight; he was small enough for me to get on top of, and putting the knife to his throat slowed any feeling of a victory he may have had.

Then I heard Thomas.

"Don't kill him!!" he shouted.

I thought about Jake then and how scared he was. But now, I could talk like I wanted to.

"You like scaring little kids, you little shit? If I catch you anywhere near me brova again, this is what will 'appen to ya," I snarled at him.

I had both of his elbows pinned by my knees so I reached down and sliced his index finger off his right hand. Thomas had showed me how to sharpen my blade with two rocks, so the blade went through his finger like a spoon in freshly mashed potatoes. He let out a large scream and I laughed so loudly. He couldn't get up and he struggled as much as he could. I was in complete control.

At that moment, Jake's hand was on my shoulder. I had never forgotten how his little hands felt on my shoulder, even after he had grown man calluses on them from working in the field with Thomas and me. I couldn't slow down my breathing; I wanted to see his throat open and feel the blood gushing all over my face. Then, Jake spoke to me.

"Remember ya promise, Troy," he whispered.

I remembered. The entire kill in me washed away instantly. I got off him, but threw his finger off in the bushes somewhere. He stood, clutching his right hand.

"Ya gonna pay fa that one ya are," the man said as he hobbled off into the woods.

"Troy-boy, how are ya?" I heard Thomas say.

I was so focused on the man leaving that Jake had to smack me across the face to get me back to normal. I finally got my breathing back to normal and the blood in my veins began to flow better through my body. I grabbed Jake and hugged him.

"Don't ever leave our sight again, you hear me Jake? People in this area don't really like your kind and you have no control over it," Thomas said. "It's not your fault, but just remember some people don't think of you and your color as equal to them, and they dislike you for that."

I looked at Thomas and I was as serious as I could be at fifteen.

"I will kill whoever tries to hurt Jake. Even if they are just scaring him. I will kill them; you understand me? I don't want to do that again, so please, I will stay at the house from now on. If you run into trouble with Jake, don't tell me about it. I will find and kill whoever tries to hurt or scare him. I don't care about meself. I just care about me brova," I said.

Thomas just nodded his head and handed me the rifle that I dropped. We walked back to the house in silence. I made sure to keep my eyes on Jake. He didn't wander too far away from us after that. But, I kept my word and never left the house when they went hunting again. Jake would go out with Thomas because he never had a father that loved him, and Thomas actually loved him. That day that we got into it with the Irish men showed me that.

December 2, 1887

So, I have finally made a name for myself. But now, I have nothing to say to Sarah. She's left me alone in this world and she knows that if I find someone that I will slowly forget about her. I think that is how she operates, but she does not understand that I wanted Tabitha physically and her (Sarah) emotionally. For Sarah, emotion is not enough. She wants blood. Sarah enjoys the killings more than I do, it seems.

I've begun to get worried after Tabitha's demise. I don't know what Sarah is doing with those auras and why they make her look more "human." Or "alive," I should say. Sarah was very much alive after Tabitha's death and I was almost confused. I want to know if she is still dead. I think that I will ignore this for a while and focus on my normal, day-to-day activities. I will kill for Sarah no longer. She will not control me as she has in the past. I will live my life as I want to.

April 05, 1888

I know I haven't written anything in a long time. But things have been a little different at this place since we first arrived. I was nervous that they gave me a name. I mean, "Jack the Ripper"? I cannot believe that was the best name that they could create. I don't see Sarah as much as I did when I was creating my artwork. I have gone almost a full five months without as much as a look at a whore who may be worth killing. I have even quit my job as a garbage man and begun a normal position as a butcher. I don't even want to walk down that infernal route anymore. I am exhausted from all of this.

Being a butcher is nice because I am still able to use a knife. For those of you who may want to question my age, I am now twenty-nine. I don't want marriage and I don't want to be with anyone. Tabitha has shown me that I don't need or want to be with anyone. I have been in the butcher's shop for at least four and a half weeks. The owner has not given me any problems. He is not the best manager, but he still makes sure that I get paid on time and gives me no real lip about anything. I still go out at night and drink, but I am not as disgusted with the interactions of the 'ladies of the night'.

Now, I have noticed some easy targets and I know Sarah would love them. So I make sure to not go after them. Sarah is highly upset. I go home and laugh. Yes, she plagues my dreams with all sorts of evil things, but that's as strong as she is. She has no real power over me, and after Tabitha, I realized this. I've even begun to show her by not committing any pieces of art. I was, at least, able to relieve some of the pain and stress that I've had from my life through Tabitha and our sexual romps. But, Sarah made sure to take that away from me. Well, that's fine; I am taking away her ability to make more 'friends'. So, I've worked tirelessly at the butcher's shop. I've obtained as many hours as I could, sometimes without pay. I don't care; I will do anything to keep my mind preoccupied; so I do not sleep. I've become an insomniac. That is until one night. I could go no further. I finally slept. All I remember was sitting on the bed and then nothing.

What I remember is riding a horse through London. Buildings were on fire from the windows. The people walking through the streets weren't really people, but some type of walking dead people. I could see their ribs or different body organs. The skyline was a dark, grayish purple. I am sure that the sky was reflecting a large ball of light at the end of the roadway. At the end of the road, there was a large, oval aura of light pulsating in and out, up and down. The horse I was on was dead as well. I had no saddle or harness, so I had to grab the mane of the horse to keep on him. When I grabbed the mane, hair came off in clumped masses and bloody, long, decayed strands. Its sides were slimy with blood and other body fluids from its skin. I was having massive trouble keeping on the wet body when it began to trot faster towards the light.

The horse started to gallop and the people around began to walk towards me in ghoulish, jerky movements. I was now hearing the voices call the ever-speeding horse towards it. The beaconing was causing the horse to breathe in raspy heaves. Every time I went to grab his body, it came off in meaty, bloody clumps. The light began to pulsate faster and faster the closer that this death steed got to it.

I didn't really know the purpose of this light, but I was not getting a good feeling from it. When I looked at the people, they were running on all fours towards us. I could feel my body begin to slip from my demonic ride. The cobblestone road was taking the click clack of the horses' hooves with no resistance. I signaled for the horse to slow down and it listened not. I finally fell off and shortly got overran by the people. The almost skinless people hoisted me over their heads. The horse stopped and turned to face me when they dropped me to its feet. I could now see it in all its grotesqueness. The monsters were holding my shoulders and arms while I knelt to the ground. I couldn't resist. I knew it was Sarah before I could see the horse's black tongue.

"No," I said.

I didn't even want to hear what she had to say.

"Troy-boy, you have no choice but to come back into the light." Her voice was, of course, not human.

She trotted over to me and licked the long horse's tongue over my face, leaving a black, sticky film. I was too weak to fight back.

"You see, my love, no matter how much you try and escape it, you will never be able to. I need you like you need me," it said.

"You will get nothing from me," I wheezed out.

For some reason, I found it hard to move and breath. I initially felt this weakening the closer to the purple light the horse took me.

"She didn't deserve you, Troy. You know that. You and I belong together forever. Isn't that what you wanted, my love?" the horse asked.

"No, not like this. You will pay for what you did to her. I will not kill for you anymore," I said back.

The horse then screamed and reared on its hind hooves, which then came down on me, and I woke up.

Sarah does not like what I am doing and I am fine with it.

"I will not do that for you anymore, Sarah," I say, looking at her in the dresser mirror across from my bed.

She has a scowl on her face from the very depths of hell.

April 07, 1888

I have been working at the market on my daily duties: cutting mutton chops and tossing out pig intestines. Today, as I was going about setting out my different meats, I saw a woman with a group of children, and for some reason, she reminds me of Ms. Applegum. They crossed the road in front of my store, Ben's Meats. I could see her through the store name painted on the window. I could only assume she was some sort of school teacher. She came into the store and the bell rang as she walked in. I flashed a welcoming smile.

"What can I help you with, ma'am?" I asked in a cheery voice.

She gave me this look of disdain. One of the little boys stepped out of line and she reached in her purse, pulled out a thick wooden ruler, and rapped him on the top of his head. His hands instantly went to the top of his head and he looked back at her. She carefully placed the ruler back into her handbag. I saw red, but I had to stay cool.

"Yes, I would like to look around for a moment please," she said with her sloppy lips.

"Looks like you have a little classroom with you," I said, looking at all the children.

"Yes, we are from the Little Yorkie Elementary School," she said.

I looked down the seven children in a straight line and they all looked as though they were in a trance of negativity. When my eyes got to the last child, I saw Sarah looking at me with her hand on the last his shoulder. She then slowly began to float up to the front of the line, placing her hand on each one. She was in her 'living' form. Had she really been alive, she would have been ruffling each child's hair. She had on a white dress and her auburn hair was flowing down her shoulders. I looked back at the poor excuse for a teacher. Sarah does not rule me anymore, so I didn't care what she thought of the situation. And then, Sarah appeared beside me, near my ear.

"What is her name?" she whispered to me.

I began to sweat, even though it was cool inside the building. Sarah knew how I felt about that ruler in her bloody purse. I wanted to break it over the lady's head. She wasn't as large as Applegum, but she had the same despicable demeanor. This lady had no moles or anything, but she had that same wrinkled, thin skin. I wish I could have sunk my butcher's knife into hers right then.

"Oh, so you are a teacher are you? That seems like a tiring job," I said.

Every time I looked at that handbag, I would see the ruler inside.

"Well, Mrs...?" I asked.

"Ms. Carlisle. I am widowed. And yes, I am these little runts' teacher," she said.

I could not look at her anymore. I removed one of the butcher's knives from its sleeve behind the counter and took it to our back sharpening room.

I sat in the chair and began to step on the manual crank of the sharpening rock and placed the edge of the blade on the stone. After five and a half months, I now have a target. I wasn't even planning on doing this anymore, but something took over me when she used that ruler on that poor boy's head. There were no words used and it really irritated me. I wanted to stop her but I had no choice but to watch as she performed the act. I continued to grind the blade down to its sharpest peak. I stopped and checked a few times to see how sharp it had become.

Sarah was in the room now. She wants her as much as I do because she hasn't fed in a long time. I laughed. Sarah has paid for what she had done to Tabitha, so now will be a good time. Ms. Carlisle will be the one who will feel my blade next. Since she is a schoolteacher, this will be another difficult painting. But, I will make sure she does not get away from me.

I heard the doorbell jingle once again. I jumped up; she couldn't leave yet. The owner of the shop was not there because he needed to get more inventory. I know now that I haven't been doing my inventory either. I went back out, and to my surprise, there was another customer inside. I glanced around and saw that the lucky Ms. Carlisle was still inside with the children and looking at different meats. I rushed to the other customer and assisted him as fast as possible, but I glanced at her periodically.

"Excuse me Sir, I think I know what I would like," she said out of her fat mouth.

"Yes, Ma'am?" I asked with a smile.

"I think I want a big, fat, juicy beef steak. I will have it with a nice side of mash tonight," she said.

I wanted to scream. I hate even touching steaks now. She will have a lot to pay for. I could feel my pants getting tighter around my hardening phallus. She licked her lips as she watched me cut the steak into a suitable size. I hated when she told me that the beef cut was too small. I imagined how she would look eating this thick cut of meat and I almost gagged.

"Yes, yes that's fine good Sir," she said.

"No problem, Ma'am. So, are you all on a field trip?" I asked, handing her the wrapped meat.

"Yes, well, I have to take the brats to see the Whitechapel Church. I'm sure that none of them will be interested anyway, but it's still a part of their learning, supposedly," she said.

One of the children said something that I couldn't hear and she reached into her purse again. I thought about cutting her hand off as soon as she withdrew the ruler from the bag.

"Well, Ma'am, enjoy your day," I interrupted.

"Of course I will, as soon as these little ratfinks go home to their mums," she said, removing her hand from the bag.

She hadn't taken her eyes off the student who caused her so much trouble. I was angery and elated at the same time. This will not be a service for Sarah. Oh no, not this one. I will do this one for the children, no, not just the children; this will be for Jake. My little brother, Jake. I am sure that he realizes why some people need to be taken from this world. I don't understand why certain people would work with children if they do not like children in the first place. It boggles me and makes me really dislike them. I watched her as she went out and Ben ran into them.

"Oi, Thomas, I need ya 'elp. Got new stock; need ya ta go 'round back and get that big door opened up." Ben said in his normal, cheery voice.

"Looked like ya had quite a crowd there, mate. I didn't know ya were servin the kiddies," he laughed.

"Oh no, she came in with her little brood," I replied.

"Oi, the lilto kiddies, aren't dey da cutest?" he said.

I know he likes kids based upon that statement. I don't have any problem with him. I need Ms. Carlisle. She needs to be done and done. I am happy to oblige her with becoming one of our art pieces. I will make sure to make the paper on this action. I'm thinking about how nice it will feel to cut into something nice and warm for a change.

"Thomas, grab that leg if ya don't moind ya willy 'ead," Ben said.

I didn't realize that I had left the moment.

"Yes, I gotcha Sir," I said.

"I told ya about that sir shite. Knock it off ya bugga! Call me Ben or ya fiored," he said back.

"Yes, Sir...er Ben," I said back. "Hey there, Ben, quick question: where is the Little Yorkie Elementary School?" I asked.

We finished placing all the odd meats back into the cold room. Ben is a good manager. He pays me well and makes sure I work decent hours. He's even given me a key to open and close the shop when I want. We had to finish with these meats before they went bad. I finished the day with Ben and headed back home.

I have to figure out how I will do this. I'm not sure that Ms. Carlisle will be out after hours. I will need to follow her after she gets off work. I'm not sure if I will have time off from work to do so. She will need to be leaving work and I have to find out where she lives to get a proper idea of how to begin my painting. The only issue is that I normally get off work at five o' clock p.m. while she may get off at two o' clock. This in itself is a dilemma. I need to find out how I can do this without causing a scene.

Sarah gives me nothing to go on. I think the only reason she was so focused on Rose was because she wanted to paint Tabitha. Therefore, I will have to do this on my own. It's not like this is the first killing that I have done on my own. And now, that fat, little Ms. Carlisle has helped me to open up a fresh itch that needs scratching.

September 17, 1867

After we arrived home from the incident, Betty grabbed Jake, kissed and hugged him. For some reason, she always had a nice piece of taffy ready for him from her and Thomas' trips into town on their little horse and carriage. I was walking in as she did this, and she looked over at me with my bloody pants leg and almost tackled me to see if I was hurt.

"What happened to you, sweet pea?" she nearly screamed.

"He's fine, but I was worried about the attacker, hon," Thomas said.

"Yeah Ma, Troy didn't kill him and I was so happy I almost cried, but I didn't, I promise," Jake said before I could say anything.

"Yeah, he did well to protect you Jake. Why don't you go on upstairs for a bit? Me, Betty and Troy-boy are going to have a little chat," Thomas said.

"He ain't in trouble is he? He didn't do nothin' but protect me," Jake said.

Betty didn't correct him this time. She was focused on Thomas and how stern his face was. Even though we had been on the farm for three years, Jake still needed my seal of approval before he made any moves. Thomas didn't want to have to repeat himself to Jake, so I figured I would step in and say something.

"Go on Jake, I knew I needed to talk to 'em. It will be okay. I will be up there before you can start a game of chess with yourself," I said.

He listened. I was so proud of him-- like a father of a son. He would play games of chess by himself to try and get better. I would laugh sometimes, but I wasn't smart enough to play the game by myself like he was. I knew that Thomas wanted to talk to me because he had been silent since we went to get the rifles and all the way back home. I think he may have been nervous about how to approach the situation or how to even approach me. He cleared his throat and pulled out a seat for Betty, then sat down next to her. He then motioned for me to sit in front of them across from the large, circular table.

"Umm... Jake is great, isn't he?" he asked.

I knew he was stalling so I decided to help him.

"Yeah, he's a great brother. I am sorry for what I did back there. I know I went too far for them just scaring him. I feel that I'm all he has and I need to keep him safe. I am very grateful for you two and what you did for us. But, I feel badly when I let him get into a bad situation and I can't protect him from it. I get angry. But, I'm not ever gonna be mad at you two. If that's what you are thinking; is that what you are thinking?" I asked.

Betty kept her eyes on me with a confused look on her face.

"No, not at all, Troy-boy. I don't think that at all. It's just that you can't just go around killing people. Sometimes a good scaring is what a lot of people need. And maybe you went just a little too far today," Thomas said.

"I'm sorry; I am a little lost, hun. What did Troy-boy do?" Betty asked.

"Umm...I can explain it to you later, dear. But let's just say someone has nine fingers instead of ten, and they now know that they cannot bother Jake anymore. I'll tell you that," Thomas said with a smile on his face. "Imma be honest with you, Troy-boy, and you know I am not a liar. I was afraid. Not for you, because the way you grabbed him I knew he didn't stand a chance against you. I was afraid for him and whether you knew how to control yourself. I understand how much you love Jake, and if someone was to do something to him, I probably would act the same way. Killing someone who does something to your family is almost understood, but for a person to scare them and you want to kill them, it may be a little extreme is all I'm saying. Understand?" He asked.

All I could do was nod. He would never understand or get me. I didn't mind as long as they kept Jake safe.

We were given night chores before we went to bed. These were the real quiet times. Thomas would be on the front porch smoking a pipe with Betty at his side in their 'his and her' rocking chairs, while Jake and I would be inside playing with water for the dishes. Every once and a while, Betty would tell us to keep it down or not to make a mess while cleaning, but we learned to clean up before they came in. We didn't really worry about punishments or anything like that, because we still would have fun. This night seemed no different. Oh, but it was.

Jake jumped when the explosion outside the barn happened, and it made him drop the plate he was holding. After the bright blast shook the windows of the kitchen, I heard Thomas and Betty on the front porch.

"Go inside and get the boys, hon. Go on now! Troy-boy, get me my rifle and you 'n Jake go with Betty upstairs- and get a hustle on it!" he screamed.

I ran to the coat rack and searched through the coats as fast as I could, but it felt like hours. I finally found the two rifles and a powder bag.

"No, Troy, you go upstairs, and if anyone of 'em get past me you can take care of that one. I don't have time to argue with you," he said after I tossed him the first rifle and powder bag.

I stood there for a moment and mulled it over, but he was right, and I still would have my knife. I was always able to protect Jake no matter what. I took the rifle upstairs with me. It had no powder or bullets in it, so I gave it to Betty. I ran down to my room, knelt under my bed and grabbed my knife. As I ran back to the room where Betty and Jake were hiding, I heard a window break downstairs.

"Someone's down there," I whispered to Betty as I came in the room and closed the door behind me.

"Umm...okay. Okay, Troy you get into the closet, and I'll lock you in. Jake, you get under the bed and it will be fine. Don't you come from under there no matter what happens, okay, Sonny? You promise me not to move until it's quiet," she whispered to us, clutching the empty rifle to her bosom.

"I can help you, though, so it won't be hard," I said.

"No! Do like I say and do it now!" she whispered as loud as she could.

I waited for her to kiss Jake and for him to roll under the bed, and then I climbed into the large wardrobe closet. She and I both knew that Jake wasn't good in enclosed places. He always seemed to bugger out if he was in a situation where he was closed in. She kissed me on the forehead and locked the door. When she pulled the key out of the keyhole she looked back in through the little hole.

"Don't worry, Troy-boy, we will be right back to get you before you know it. Please be quiet. Don't make a sound," she whispered.

I watched through the key hole and saw her standing at the door with the rifle as a club to the left of the door. The footsteps had gotten to the door and she tensed up. The door was kicked in and she miscalculated her swing, only to hit the door frame. The man from the woods grabbed her, smacked her to the ground then kicked her in the chest. There was nothing she could do at that point. He had a short cut with a small mustache. He was a red head. I had never seen a man with red hair before. He knelt down and snatched her hair back.

"Where is the lito fuzzy? Hmm....Where is the nigger?" he asked in his funny accent.

The second man from the woods walked in at that time, crouched next to them, and licked her face with a haggard laugh.

The first man looked at him and laughed. "Check the closet, wud ya?" he said.

He then turned Betty over and began to punch her. I could almost hear Jake fidgeting. The second man walked over and tried to open the door.

"Bullocks, it's locked!" he said.

"Foind da key then, ya ape!" Man One said.

"No wait, he's under the bed!" Betty cried out.

"No!" I yelled, punching the closet door.

Man Two turned back to the wardrobe closet I was in.

"Ah, we got our lilto Finga Cutta. Manny wants this one too," Man Two said, walking to the bed.

He lifted the whole bed and Jake darted for the door. I couldn't see it all, but Man One had him. Jake was able to get one hard jab off before the man grabbed his wrist and pulled his twelve-year-old body in a crude chokehold. While Jake gagged and tears began to stream down his face, Man Two picked Betty up off the floor.

"Hey there Finga Cutta, lookie hea, mate," he said.

He pulled out a large hunting knife and slit her throat. The last thing I saw her say was "sorry." Jake tried to scream. In that moment, I felt she deserved it. Had they not done it, I would have. She had this all planned.

133

Jake should have been in this closet. I would have used my knife and kept us safe like Thomas told me. She had given up Jake because he was easier to watch die than me.

"We're gunna burn ya aloive!" he said

"Fokin shite, Harold, what dija do 'at for?" Man One said, nudging Harold.

"Fought 'at's wot Manny wonted," Harold said.

"Yea, but we coulda had sum fun wiv her first," Man One said.

They dropped Betty on the ground as the last of her useless life left her. I don't know when I began kicking the door, but I went hoarse screaming for Jake. They dragged Jake away while he struggled for air. His little body flailed around as he tried to escape.

"C'mon mate, we gotta stort the foire," Man One said.

Harold followed. I struggled with the door for a little longer and after I smelled the smoke, I accepted my fate. I realized I was going to die there.

"But what about Jake?" I asked in my empty tomb.

I can rock this wardrobe! I thought. I began to shake the would-be coffin back and forth until it finally fell forward with a loud crack! The wood splintered up the side like a lightning strike. I gave two more solid kicks and an opening big enough for me to crawl through appeared. I made my way out of the room and ran to the doorway where Betty lay with her eyes opened. I spat on her and stepped out.

Smoke filled the upstairs and red orange licks of fire were all along the bottom floor. My thoughts were everywhere. My mind would not focus on one thing at all. I did remember that there was a tree that Jake and I would

134

climb out of on some nights. I had tears in my eyes and I did not know if it was from the smoke or the fact that I let Jake down again. The dry wood made the fire move a lot faster than I could almost escape. I made it out the window before I began to see it peek around the door of my former room.

I heard the horse and carriage leave as I climbed down the tree from my window. I rounded the corner, and from the light of the burning house and barn, I saw Thomas on his stomach with a bullet hole in his back. I could see his breathing was not normal. Someone had surprised him from behind. Those bastards. I ran over to him.

"Thomas, c'mon mate, let's get up!" I shouted to him.

I could tell he was having a hard time getting out what he needed to say. I tried to hold back the tears as he barely inhaled. He was as weak as I had ever seen him.

"Sa...save...Jake," he sputtered.

"Where is he? Where did ya see 'im?" I asked.

Thomas lifted one hand and barely pointed out into nothingness. His hand wobbled and his finger barely straightened. I tried to follow his hand in the night to where he was pointing. As I walked over, I heard dripping noises as I stepped into a wet patch of grass. The dripping stopped and I felt something warm on the top of my head. I looked up and fell to my knees while tears streamed uncontrollably from my eyes. There, on the bottom branch of the tree, hung my little brother. At twelve years old, he had no chance against the grown men. I shouted and shouted into the night with no one to answer me. His little stomach had been cut from the belly button to the top of his neck and his intestines were used as a crude rope to hang him. They had gutted him like a sick animal.

From what I saw in the darkness, his little innards were stretched around his modest throat. I could tell from the flickering flames that his eyes were bloodshot red. He had no chance, and I was not there to even attempt to protect him. I looked back at Thomas and his eyes reflected the fire back at me, not blinking once. I knew what that meant. I sat under that tree and cried for hours. I could not stop even after I cut him down and buried Thomas next to him. I lay next to them that entire night and slept.

The next morning, I could only think about the two names I had embedded into my mind. I began looking around the path to the major road and followed the horse hooves. The only repayment I could think of for this was blood. I needed it. That was the only thing that would sedate my rage. I knew I would laugh as I was doing the same to them as they had done to Jake. I had no food or water; all I had was my knife and the two names. Manny and Harold. I walked through the woods chanting their names, over and over, into the darkness.

April 12, 1888

I used my lunch hours to go to her job and look at the scenery of the school. I wanted to know how I would be able to kill someone during the day. So, over the past few weeks, I was friendly enough with Ben that he allowed me to take my lunch breaks whenever I wanted to take them. Some days, I took them at one o' clock and waited until the school let out. I needed to know when she got off. Yet, this began to take up too much of my time. I had to go back to the drawing board and figure out a new method of acting out my plans.

After lunch last week, I walked into work and Ms. Carlisle walked right past me with another wrapped piece of meat. I'm almost sure it was a steak.

"Well hello, Sir. I was looking for you. I sneaked away from work for a second to get me another of those juicy steaks you cut me last time," she said. "What's your name? I want to ask for you specifically-- because the other gentleman did not give me the same cut that you gave me last time."

She was a greedy one, she was. I was upset and shocked to see her at this time of day. I glanced down at her handbag and knew that her ruler was in there and it made me angry. I hid it pretty well.

"Yes, Ma'am, you can ask for Mr. Wilschire. I'll be there to help-- no problem," I said with a labored smile.

"Yes, well don't worry Mr. Wellshir, I will definitely ask for you by name," she said, walking past me.

I was boiling. The dumb whore could not even pronounce my name correctly. The only reason that I cut the steaks so large was because I wanted to get rid of the horrible things.

"Ya made some sorta impression on 'at la'ee roight there," Ben said when I entered the shop.

"Yeah, I try to do the best that I can. I didn't know that she liked steaks so much," I said.

Then I figured it out. Right then and there on the spot. I figured out what I would do to this woman who eats steaks like they are pieces of candy. I would feed her all the candy she could take. Poison! I would poison the beef before I gave it to her. She couldn't eat the disgusting meat before a certain time of day. I couldn't help but laugh aloud. I laughed to tears while Ben wondered what my angle was.

"What's on ya, mate?" Ben said.

"Oh nothing, just thinking of a joke a man told me on the way here," I said quickly.

"No worries, mate. I'm not the joking type," he said.

I just needed to do more research to find out what I could use that she would not smell or taste until it was too late. Like good ole Jeremiah, Ms. Applegum, and my mum. Upon leaving work, I went by one of the local bookstores to look up different poisons and how they would affect a person's body. I figured I would stick with the old faithful arsenic. It works well when used in abundance. Now, all I needed to do was give her the meat infused with the poison and she would be gone from this world with that silly little ruler of hers.

I asked Ben to show me how he salts the meats for storage. And he happily showed me. See, the good thing about Ben is that he looks at me like a son, being that his had not followed his footsteps and done the butcher thing. But that's neither here nor there. Ms. Carlisle had my full attention. I couldn't wait to read in the paper what happened to her. So, after learning the infusion process, I waited until I could get down her pattern of movements. I spoke and made small conversation with her whenever I saw her. I got angrier and angrier every time she asked me to lengthen her cut of meat.

Today, I finally had the set up. This morning, I took the meat that would be 'seasoned' to the back of the meat area where we prepare the big pieces. Early in the morning, Ben comes in off a fresh hangover and sleeps in the back of the packaging area. I went there and infused the meat with the arsenic. It took me a while to obtain the poison since it was found in rat killer. But, it's fine. I like this method a little better because the 'Ripper' will not be the blame for this one.

The only thing that Sarah and I are upset about is that we will not be able to see her vomit up the chunks of steak and her side dish. I want to see her eyes run with the tears of why her body was rejecting her normal treat. I smiled when I injected the meat with more of the liquefied death.

I waited until she came in with the two students who she was keeping from fighting each other with her ruler in hand. I knew this would be the last time she would use that horrid tool. So, my smile today was a little brighter knowing this.

"Hello there, Mr. Welpshirt," she said incorrectly.

"Yes, hello Ms. Carlisle. How are you today?" I said brightly.

"Yes, I would like to look around for a bit," she said.

I hated her for this. She would always do such silly things as though she did not know what she wanted. I would always walk up and down the aisle with her until she figured out what she wanted-- which was always the *damn steak*. She finally settled on something and I already assumed it was the lovely steak. I didn't mind cutting the steak this time, for I knew it would be put to good use.

"Yes Mr. Wiltskirt, I will take the slab of bacon. I feel as though I have had enough steak for a while. I don't know if I should be eating that much cow," she said.

She knew. I didn't know what to say for a few moments.

"Mr. Wetshin. Did you hear me?" she asked.

I could not believe that out of all the times to choose a meat she ended up choosing bacon? I was so infuriated. Maybe she knew what my plans were. She was trying her best to take me out of character to expose myself.

"Uh, no steak today, huh?" I asked.

Every day she comes in to get the steak and she chose, today of all days, not to get it.

"Oh no, I think my brother will be in town and I only need some bacon for our breakfast when he arrives," she said with a smile.

"Okay, no problem," I said, cutting the bacon to her wishes.

She did her normal routine of asking for a bigger cut and I wrapped the meat up for her and gave her the price after weighing it.

"Well, Ms. Carlisle, I don't want you to miss out on the fresh beef that we have in stock, and since you are such a valued customer I will throw in a free steak for you," I said. Service with a smile.

I didn't care that I would have to pay for the meat myself, because her choking death would be enough payment for me. I ran to the back and picked up the specially flavored cut of beef for her greedy little mouth.

"Oh my, thank you so much, Mr. Williams. That is very kind of you. I was going to have soup tonight but now I will have me this nice cut of steak. Thank you again," she said gleefully.

I smiled back at her. Maybe she was unsure or did not know that I was planning her demise the whole time.

"No need to thank me, Ms. Carlisle. I just want you to tell me how much you enjoyed it tomorrow. That will be thanks enough for me," I said.

"I think a good searing on each side will do this wonderfully," she said. "I like to have as much redness as I can in the center." She licked her lips as she said this. At this point, I just wanted her out of the store.

"Yes, that sounds delicious. You will just die after eating this cut of meat. I had some myself last night," I lied to her. My stomach began to turn as soon as I thought of the rough meat.

She finally left, and a few moments later, Ben came from the back of the store. It was around one thirty at this time. Ben was a short, chubby, balding man who drank a lot but was still cheerful.

"Oi, many customers there, Thomas?" he asked.

"Oh no, just the right amount, Ben," I smiled.

"Well, since ya worked the majority o' the day, ya can take the rest of the day off. I'll pay ya for the whole thing," he smiled.

"Why thanks a lot, Ben. Just let me clean up the rest of all this and I'll be out of your hair," I said.

I was able to sneak in the special meat in with Ms. Carlisle and leave work early. It was a wonderful day indeed.

April 13, 1888

Today, I had to continue doing my daily duties in the butcher's market after Ben came in to do his normal sleeping until twelve or one. I couldn't wait until the paper boy shouted out his normal 'GET YA PAPER ROIGHT 'ERE!' shout. As soon as I heard it, I ran outside and purchased a paper. I franticly got back into the store and flipped through the papers. I was sure it would have been on the front page. But for some reason it wasn't. I did not understand.

"Lookin fo tha funnies, Thomas?" Ben asked.

"Uh. No not at all. Just checking for the birthdays," I said.

Where the hell is the story of her death? I can't believe it. Why wasn't she on the front page? I handled the situation correctly to my knowledge. But, wait…I didn't handle it correctly. I didn't handle it at all. I didn't actually *do* the killing myself. No, that means nothing. She just hasn't been found. I will just wait a few days and we will see what happens. I feel Sarah chomping at the bit to find out what happens. I'm not really upset at this point, but I know that I just need to wait.

April 15, 1888

Today, after getting everything cleaned, I saw across the street and through the window Ms. Carlisle! I thought I was in a dream. I began to get nervous. I knew that she had found out about the poison in the steak. I was very antsy to find out what she wanted. I could feel my hands begin to sweat and my hairs on the back of my neck stand up. I headed to the back from where I got her 'seasoned' steak. I stood over the sterile table as my mind raced and heart began its hop skip in my chest. I know I put plenty of arsenic in the meat because I put less in my mother's mash if I remember correctly. The bell at the top of the door rang.

"Mr. Welstir, Mr. Welster!" she called from the front.

I didn't have a clue of what to do. I stood there, looking at the dead cow on the table. If she found out about the poisoned meat, I would be done for. I was not really worried, though, because I would just take a cleaver to her forehead. This made me smile because I could actually see her demise. I reached up to the top of the hanging rack and brought out the largest cleaver we had. This was used to cut up all the heavy carcasses and to get through bones.

"Give me on second, please!" I shouted out to the front.

"I am late for work and I must speak with you please," she said impatiently.

I walked out with a smile on my face and the cleaver underneath my white apron.

"Well hello, Ms. Carlisle. What can I help you with, madam?" I said, smiling.

"Yes, well thank you very much for the meats the other day. But I do have a quandary about the steak," she said suspiciously.

She knew. I felt my hands around the cleaver gripping tighter. There is a large, half oval glass that we display different selections of meats in. And for some god forsaken reason, she always wants to keep her hands on the fucking glass. I have to wipe it constantly to keep the glass clean so that other customers won't think that we are some sort of second rate business whenever she leaves.

"Oh, well what happened?" I asked.

"Well nothing bad, I was just so happy with the cut I ended up giving it to my brother. My question to you is, is there any way that I can get another cut like that?" she asked.

I could have laughed aloud. I was so sure that she wanted to report me or accuse me of poisoning the steak. So, to hear her ask for another cut of meat because she gave the poisoned piece to her brother, I felt the need to uncontrollably laugh. This silly bitch did not even realize the plans that I had for her, and she wanted to come and beg for more food. Sarah began to whisper in my ear. I finally had a perfect way of getting this art piece on my mantle easier than I thought.

"Well, we do have a program where we can actually deliver the meats to your home. I could definitely throw in some extra here and there when the boss isn't looking," I said. I whispered the last part as though she was really getting a deal."

See, here at Ben's Butchers, we obtain more meat then we know what to do with. Sometimes we need to throw it away. I am certain that I will be able to get parts from the throwaway area, make a move to her home, and perform my work of art there. I will even be happier with this because I will be able to actually see what the art piece looks like.

I began to get even more excited about the whole situation than she was. I could see from the way her face brightened up that she was excited, but needed to think it over a while.

"Yes, well I think I would like that, Mr. Wiltsky. If you could, can you please make sure that the meat is cut in nice, big, juicy pieces like that last steak you cut for me?" she asked greedily.

I ripped off a piece of paper that we use for receipts and gave her a pen. Set a trap for the rabbit and they are bound to go in, simply out of curiosity. She was curious to see what I would provide for her and I smiled as she jotted down her address.

"But of course, Ms. Carlisle. I will be sure to make the best cuts on you." I said with confidence.

"Excuse me, Mr. Wilter?" she asked, surprised.

"Yes Ms. Carlisle?" I replied.

"Oh, it sounded like you said 'on' me. I'm sure it was a slip of the tongue," she laughed.

"Yes of course, yes, I meant for you," I said.

I was so caught up in my thoughts I may have exposed myself. But, it matters not because I will still be able to paint my picture the way I want. Sarah feels as though she is back in my good graces because I could feel her caressing the back of my neck. I almost snickered as Ms. Carlisle walked out the door. The bell must have woken up Ben. He walked out, wiping his eyes.

"Top of tha morn," he said.

It was two o'clock pm. In my excitement, I was too focused on what I would do to Ms. Carlisle to even notice him standing beside me and tying his apron.

"Oh yes, good morning Ben," I said. I am so used to his daily routine that I don't even remember when I began to agree with him on the time of day.

My weekend will be spent at my second place, the cottage, where I have all the bodies buried and other tools for my artwork. Ben and I finished our normal Friday and I went home.

Tonight, I will go out and find where little Ms. Carlisle dwells and who with- if anyone. Finding this woman has given me a newfound reason for creating more of the artwork that Blacksmith calls a crime. I smell Sarah as she flows in and out of my mind. I always feel as though she likes to mull about in my memories throughout the day.

September 17, 1867

I walked for miles that night. I stopped a couple of times to drink from a creek or to try and eat some fruits from a couple of farms that I may have passed. I had even made a rabbit trap from what Thomas had taught me. Set the trap and they will enter. I finally made it to a small town. I had lost the killers' tracks hours ago. I just needed to keep walking. Things had become desperate, and I would resort to begging here and there. A few people offered to take me in, but I refused. I didn't want to become close with anyone else. I had lost too much already.

There were nights when I remember just crying about the things that Thomas had taught me or things that Jake and I had laughed at while we were supposed to be asleep at night. I think around this time is when I started to hear my mother's voice. She would seem to guide me. It only started out as whispers the first few times. She would tell me little things in my dreams. In one dream, she apologized for how she treated me. In another, she told me that I deserved what I got at the orphanage. I didn't know what to believe.

I was more concerned with Manny and Harold. I was able to read little snippets of their attacks, in used papers, on people that were definitely weaker than they were. I was so angry at the fact that they listed Thomas and Betty in there with the weak ones. Thomas wasn't weak at all. And that is what really pissed me off the most. I knew that Thomas was smarter than them and I knew he could have handled all three or four of the men of ill refute when I met him, and even more so when I saw how he protected Jake. My poor, poor brother. I hated myself for not being there for him. And that bitch Betty allowed him to get killed. She actually gave him up. I wish I could have felt my blade across her snake of a neck. If anything, she killed him herself.

My mother laughed in my head at times when I cried about Jake. She was despicable to me, even after death. She would laugh and jeer about how Betty showed her true colors at the end and how I was the fool for believing that she had loved Jake and me as a mother loves her children. I would read on about the killers to see that they were trying to be a negative influence on people by bringing in anyone who was Irish into what they were calling a "mob." It was four of them who had done what they did to the closest thing I could call a family. I would make sure to take their families from them.

The last area that I saw they were in or near was about ten miles south of where I was. My mouth began to water when I read how close they were to me. I tossed the paper to the ground, found a piece of bread in a trash barrel and began my trek towards South London. I rubbed my knife's edge until I felt the wetness of blood in my pocket as I walked into the dark alley leading to the outer part of the town, but no one would see it in the shadows. No one would see me in the obscurity. I snickered as the darkness of the alley shrouded me. My mother was silent.

April 17, 1888

This weekend, I will make sure to make the best of my time. The cottage is located on the west outskirts of London, and I have to get to the east side to do my investigations. It's not really that difficult to do, I just want it to go smoother. I have to get back into London before I can get an actual carriage to get close to her home. Then walk the rest of the way. The problem is that carriages are hard to come by at night after a certain time. But that isn't important. I know that I will have to do this anyway. This artwork will be special. I was not able to really paint Ms. Applegum like I wanted to, but Ms. Carlisle will be one that everyone will look at as a work of art—I will make sure of it.

On my way to her house today, I took out the little piece of paper from my jacket pocket and under the street lanterns, I was able to read what I needed from it. I guess I will live up to my name with her. Ms. Carlisle won't be able to come in and order the steak with that stupid ruler in her handbag anymore. As I got closer to the address, I saw there was a nice-sized home with many large windows. I am already vexed. Someone may see the artwork before I get finished and I am not happy with that.

I needed to see what else could be done. I had to duck down behind some bushes due to her coming to the window to do something. I could not really see what she was doing. I squatted and walked around the side of the house. I was trying to get a better view--to see a good place to paint. I could see through the bushes that she appeared to be washing something. I checked my pocket watch and saw that the time was ticking away. I would have to walk all the way back to the cottage. But that was fine. It looks as though she is alone this weekend. The lights went out except one, and it was a small lantern that she and her cat used to walk upstairs with.

She had to have a cat, of course. She is the cat type. I am glad that I was able to see her while she couldn't see me. I went around the home after I knew she was no longer visible. I didn't want to stay there too long, so I made my way back to the outskirts of London. When I got back to my cottage hideaway, I read the files of murders that were committed in broad daylight. I enjoy the knife sharpening times because I can rub the granite stones together for hours and just think. She needs to be surprised. Just as Rose had been. I laugh at Sarah as she floats in front of me in her black dress and scaly skin. She is pleased with me now that I am back to work.

May 05, 1888

I've given it a good three weeks to make sure that she is alone on the weekends that I do not need to work. For the most part, it's just her and her cat. She comes in and asks about her meat delivery. I have to continue to stall her. I don't want to get her weekends confused or anything of that nature. So finally, after the third weekend, I saw her come in as if she was frustrated with me.

"Well, hello, Ms. Carlisle, I was just waiting for you to get here," I said as she walked in.

"Yes, well, Mr. Wilcurt, I assumed that you wouldn't be coming with any meats, so I would like to get some things for this weekend," she said angrily.

I could tell she was under the impression that I was pulling her leg again.

"Oh no, Ms. Carlisle, I just needed to make sure that the shipment that we brought in was fresh enough to be delivered to you on Saturday," I said, smiling.

She looked around the store for a short while.

"Well fine, I will be home alone on Saturday so that will be fine. I hope you don't have a problem with cats," she said.

"Oh no, I have no problem with cats. I will be in and out of your hair before you know it," I said.

"Okay, Mr. Weltcut. If I do not see you, I will be reporting this to the manager. I have waited almost four weeks for these meats you promised me," she said with a small grin on her face.

I nodded my head as she turned and left the establishment. I will make sure that she is not dissatisfied with my performance. Neither she nor Sarah will be worried about what this outcome will be anymore. Her meats and my cleaver will be delivered tomorrow with no prejudice.

I took a white apron home while on my lunch break. I also "borrowed" a large cleaver from the building. On Fridays, Ben really does not mind too much what I do, and inventory isn't done until the following Tuesday. He stays drunk enough that he will not miss the cleaver until he has to actually work. When I got back, I took out the meat I will take to her home and bagged it up. Ben leaves early every Friday since I've gained his trust, so this is no different.

This was the hardest part of my artwork because I needed to carry such a large sack home. But, after I complete my artwork with Ms.

Carlisle, I will need to have a smaller number of things with me. So, I've decided to take fewer meats than I was originally going to take with me. Now, I am ready for my painting on the morrow.

Before leaving work, I carefully packed my things in a nice sack and walked out of the door, carefully blowing out all the lamps that kept us lit at night. I am pleased with how things are going for this art piece. Ms. Carlisle is none the wiser of her imminent doom.

Since I've been home, I've come up with a plan that will surely make it so that I can get inside her home and escape the scene of my artistry before anyone sees me. If I am able to get in and out fast, I will be fine. I know that she will not have company, because I've waited outside to see if there's anyone that she's frequently had at her home over the past two weekends.

Sarah is here for me now. She is all that I have and need. I have actually begun to see her beauty again. Her normal ghastly form is not as bad as it used to be when this all began. I want her now to know I want her for my wife. That's right, I am ready to marry Sarah and all that comes with her whorish ways. What am I saying right now? For all I know, I am already insane and Sarah is just a figment of my sanity that is already lost, a whisper of my past time when I was actually sane.

I am sorry-- let me get back to my plans for this woman. I am laughing as I record this now. As I was saying, I've made it back to my room and have begun sharpening the large butcher's blade I absconded from the shop. I've wrapped the blade with a leather sheath and tied it to the meats. I'm laying back in the bed after this is completed. I can't help but chuckle at how interesting tomorrow will be. My eyes are closing and I'm about to drift away.

May 06, 1888

I must apologize about the other night and my silly conversation about marrying Sarah. After all, she is only a ghost. Nothing that can be touched, anyway. How I wish I could feel her touch. Nonetheless, I awoke this morning with a little more spry in my step. I left the building as normal in my white apron and with the meat and cleaver tucked neatly under my armpit. The cleaver, in its sheath, was easy to keep without cutting me. I did not hail a carriage, but walked down different alleyways that people rarely travel. I had the key to the market with me as well.

I made my way through the back alleys to a side way to her home so that I would not be easily seen from the main road. I squatted down below the same set of bushes I watched her from at night for at least an hour. I put my gloves on my hands quietly. I watched as she made what I assume was a cup of tea and sat at the table reading what I can also assume was the paper. She had an open yard layout and I went to her back door, making sure no one saw me. I gave three quick knocks on the door and she began to plod her large mass towards the door.

"I'm coming, I'm coming," she said.

When she opened the door, she was in a robe with a sleeping or evening gown on underneath.

"Oh, *hello* there, Mr. Welpins," she said, out of breath. "Do come in, kind sir."

I stepped in through the doorway with the package of meat in hand.

"It's Wilschire, ma'am," I said calmly.

I was not in a smiling mood and I could see she noticed. Her hand holding the tea began to shake somewhat. She stepped aside anyway and allowed me in. She directed me toward the kitchen area to place the meat down that she could not wait to tell me how to cut, no doubt. When I placed the package on her counter, she saw the knife.

"Good Lord, Mr. Weltsher. That is a large cutting tool for such a small piece of meat," she said.

She was so bewildered and had no idea what was about to happen to her.

"Yes, Ms. Carlisle. Again, my name is Wilschire, and I plan to cut the meat for you so that it may be stored properly," I said, taking off the twine that was keeping the package closed.

When the paper opened, the cat instantly jumped on the table to see what it could get from the smells on the package. The funny thing was the cat looked at me *and* Sarah. It actually followed Sarah and hissed at her. Sarah did the same.

"Oh, Mr. Pudding, this is my friend and you don't have to be so scared around him," she said. But the cat wasn't scared at all. She was just too focused on the food to sense the danger she was in.

My heart began to flutter as I knew that I was close to painting another wonderful picture. I did not have a set plan on what I was going to do, but I knew for a fact that I wanted that right hand. And she needed to be alive to see it leave her body.

"Yes, well would you like a spot of tea Mr. Wel—I'm sorry Wilschire?" she asked.

I did not want anyone who may view this artwork to think someone else was there, so I could not accept the gratuity from her.

"No thank you, Ms. Carlisle, I want to hurry and get to work this morning. I plan on cleaning the shop and needed to get this to you so that you would no longer think that I was not going to keep my word," I said calmly.

I was surprised at how calm I was. My heart was racing, yet my breathing had not increased. I think I am getting pretty good at this.

"Oh yes, of course; I understand. Now, what would you like me to do, sir?" she asked.

"Well, if you don't mind, can you please just hold the paper so that I don't accidently cut the paper along with the meat?" I replied.

And the trap was set.

"Yes, yes, of course I will. That is a trifle. I surely don't mind at all good sir," the silly rabbit said.

She began to hold the paper with her left hand, but the other side curled up. She had to finally put her teacup down and use her right hand. I picked up the blade, which seemed surprisingly light in my hand.

"Now, Ms. Carlisle, how much would you like me to cut up for you?" I said.

"Oh, well I would like about that much. I can store the rest of it," she said, pointing to half.

I raised the blade over my head and brought it down on her right hand. The cut got most of her fingers and half of her thumb. The table was flooded with dark red as the blood coursed from the fresh slice. The only piece left when she came up, with a large howl, was her pinky. The surprised face that she made was utterly indescribable. The pinky dangled from her now missing hand like a shoestring from a broken shoe. I grabbed her wrist, put it back on the table, and took the rest with the butcher's knife. For some reason, I saw the two pieces of her hand next to the meat on the wax paper and I became hysterical with laughter. She continued to scream. This made me swipe the blade across her throat.

"You will never strike Jake with that hand again, you bitch!" I said to her.

She turned in her large kitchen to try and run down her hallway. She nearly fumbled over her table in the process. When she turned her back to me, I quickly squatted down and cut her tendon on the back of her ankle and she tumbled to the tiled floor. She was now crawling through the blood-soaked floor as she tried to get to the back room. For what I do not know, but her crawling and grunting made me laugh. I placed a foot on the back of her neck and raised the bloody blade over my shoulder.

"I hope you enjoyed all the steaks that I cut for you, Ms. Carlisle. The whole time you were coming into that shop, you did not know my name. And to think you will remember it in the afterlife. I know you will because Sarah will make sure you do." I laughed. "The name is Wilschire!" I yelled, bringing the blade down into her back repeatedly.

The first strike hit her in one of her ribs instantly, splitting the bone through her back as it broke. I lost count after the third strike because she had stopped making any noises at that point. I don't know where her cat ran off to, but I needed to complete this and I did not remember bringing my small knife. I looked over to her counter because I was sure she had something. I looked down and my apron was saturated with her new warmth. I could taste the rustiness of her blood. The sweat from my forehead was stinging my eyes but I didn't feel it.

I was so happy at the meaty mess that I saw on the floor in front of me. But back to the counter-- as I searched, there was nothing. I stepped off her and went over to the drawers where she should hold something. Sarah pointed to one of the drawers and floated over to her body. She could not wait to do what she does. I still don't understand that thing. It looks as though it makes her more youthful, but she wasn't old when I killed her.

At any rate, I went to the place she pointed to and found a little knife to cut her from her rectum hole to the side of her thigh on either side. I don't know why I make these cuts this way. Sarah just gives me these ideas, or do I give them to myself? I cannot tell anymore. I didn't know how long it took me to do this but I knew I needed to leave as soon as possible. I just wanted to relish in what I had done to her.

See, in my mind, I have freed her. She is no longer bound by the chains of being someone as evil as she has been. She is now more useful by being with Sarah. Sarah is happy, so it works out perfectly fine. I have come to the realization that it is only Sarah and me now. I began cleaning everything. I rinsed off her knife and cleaned her flesh from her blade. Then I decided to take it with me anyway. I carefully wrapped her hand, along with the meat, back into the wax paper. I tied it as I did the night before with the twine and the butcher's knife. I looked around to see if there was anything that could have been left behind, and I saw nothing.

I locked the back door and climbed out of her back window. I took the same back alleys toward my home, but made a detour to the Butcher's Market. On the way, I tossed the meat along with her hand in an empty trash barrel and made my way to my place of work. I heard the familiar ringing of the bell and made my way to the back where we cut the larger meats. This area is away from the view of customers because we don't want to hurt their little eyes with the sight of what is done to the meats before we place them in the front display case. I scrubbed, as well as I could, my apron, face, and arms. Then suddenly, I heard the front bell ring. I could not believe that in my haste I forgot to lock the bloody door.

"Helloooo??" I heard from the front.

My eyes were wide, yet all the light escaped me. I could tell that voice was familiar. *Aw, bloody hell*, I thought, it was old man Gurt looking for more morning sausage. I was sweating from the top of my bald head. I reached under the cool water, got two handfuls, and splashed it on to my face and head. The stinging of the coolness snapped me back into reality. I needed to answer.

"Yes, give me a moment!" I yelled back.

I came out to see Mr. Gurt wearing his triple-thick bifocals and grey hair coming from his nose and ears. The majority of his hair is gone from the top but the sides have a little grayish black ring which go around to the back of the head. I glanced over his shoulder and saw the sun peek over a building in front of me as some type of other worldly game of hide and go seek that it was playing with someone of a higher power.

"Good morning, Mr. Gurt; how can I assist you on this fine day?" I said.

He stared at me, blinking a few times as though he didn't recognize me.

"Well, good morning to you too, young man. I think I would like half a pound of breakfast sausage. I normally don't see you all open on Saturdays. Is this some new hour thing?" he asked.

"No, I just came in to do some cleaning. But let me get you this sausage," I said.

I gathered myself and weighed him up what he needed and came around the counter with it.

"Here you go. I won't charge you for this today-- just have a nice morning," I said, rushing him out of the building.

"Well, I would like to pay, young man," he responded.

"No it's fine, Mr. Gurt, have a wonderful day please. That will be my payment," I said back to him.

He went out of the door and stood there for a moment. I locked the door and returned to the back. I had a lot of cleaning to do and I could not waste it on an old man. I took my soiled apron and shirt, wrapped it up in a fair amount of wax paper, placed it in a bag and walked out the door. This time, I remembered to lock the door behind me. I cannot wait to read the paper to find out who and what they will say about my right hand missing artwork. But, it is not a problem. I will wait. It may take a few days for them to find the body. I do not care; someone will eventually find it.

May 09, 1888

Today, I came to work at a great time. I was energized and ready. There wasn't a soul to bother me in the world. It was as if my completing the artwork on Saturday was enough for me to take back up more paintings, or sculptures, if you will. The savageness of what I completed will give me laughs for a long time. And, when I see Sarah now, she is very pleased with me. She knows that soon the paper will show the murder and she will know that it is known. I now realize that she is only excited about the murders when they are well known or seen.

At any rate, I was still in my thoughts this morning when I heard the paperboy at the end of the road yelling about the new paper. Since it was early, I went ahead and walked down to obtain a paper, knowing full well that by today they would not have found the woman's body. I went to get one anyway. When I read the headline I could not believe my eyes.

LETTERS FROM JACK THE RIPPER HAS SCOTLAND YARD BAFFLED

I was enraged. Who would actually take credit for *my* artwork?? I almost ripped the paper in half on the way back to work as I read the inked pages. They were making a yarn of what I was doing. These "murders," as they called them, had a reason. I hated the people I was after. And they deserved what they received. Now they are permanently embedded in history. Their names will be heard forever. Now, some silly, small-minded impersonator will take credit for my artwork? No. Sarah will help me understand.

I reached the door to work and the bell rang as I walked in. The paper was under my left arm and I walked behind the counter with a smile on my face. Mimicry is the best form of flattery. I must remember this. I don't know when, but I think I will write a letter as well. This may make me feel better, almost as if I will be confessing everything to Scotland Yard. If I write a letter, I may as well turn myself in. I mean, then at least they can call me Troy the Ripper instead of that stupid Jack. At the same time, Troy *did* have his days of ripping. Better yet, they will remember me as 'Finga Cutta.'

October 01, 1867

I walked for what seemed like weeks. Nourishment was very difficult to find. I knew I needed to find shelter, food, and warmth soon or I would not survive long. I arrived in the small town at night and almost fainted in an alley. This wasn't the wooded area I was used to where the things I needed were easily found. Searching through a few of the trash barrels, I would find things like half of an old eaten sandwich and older beans. I did not care at the time how old they were or what made the bread soggy. I was ravished.

One day, after eating what I could without vomiting, I found a doorway to sit in. It was semi-warm, so I squeezed into the smelly, wet corner of the door as much as I could, ignoring the urine stench, and I wept. I missed Jake, Thomas, and even my mother. I would have even settled for that whore Betty. The more I thought of Jake, the more tears poured from my eyes. I sat in the alley, going through my sorrows, and the door I was leaning on gave way, or it was opened from the other side. I no longer even thought about grabbing my knife before my right hand was on the hilt. And, it was out of my waistband nicking my hip in the process. In front of me stood the largest black man I had ever seen.

"Oi there, litlo one, 'ave you been the one at's been tearin' through me trash?" he said with a thunderous breath.

He was wearing a bar apron and had short, scruffy hair like Jake's, yet he had some twisted into thick tendrils. He had small eyes and his tongue was very thick so all his 's' sounds came out like 'sh'. He smelled like cooked meat and cleaning liquids.

"So, ya plan ta gut ole Reggie wif that tooth pick a yours?" he laughed, eyeballing my weapon.

He stood there for a moment and made a large grunting sound, which made me jump. He seemed to size me up, then slung a sack of trash out the door and closed it. He then sat down on a stack of crates. His very large belly hung between his legs. He reached his fat fingers on to a shelf beside him, revealed a rather generous sandwich, and took a large bite from it.

"What's ya name, munchkin?" he asked with food flying from his mouth as he spoke.

He had large spaces in between his teeth, so it wasn't too hard to see why this was happening. I slid the knife back into my waistband but kept my hand on the end for safe measure. I was now able to assess my surroundings and saw that I was in what resembled a cooking area, but I couldn't be sure.

"This here is Ray's Tavern, mate," he said as though he could read my mind.

"I serve some of da foinest beans and mash this side of London. You look loike ya can do wif a meal or two yasself. Me names Raymond by the way, but most of these wankers call me Reggie on account of some fool coming in here and startin' all that," he laughed and expelled gas at the same time.

I was disgusted. But, hunger has a way of overtaking one's disgust at certain times.

"Me names Tr-Thomas. Thomas Wilschire. I have no coin or any family and no place to stay," I said.

I don't have a clue why I took Thomas' name. I missed him so much, so I figured this was the only way to honor him. I knew this way I could always at least still hear his name.

"And yes, I am very hungry. I can help you out in your kitc--"

"Tavern, mate. It's a tavern. 'Ere's the thing, I can't have ya being seen due ta not having the litlo ones working loike slaves. Ya are tall enough to go for I'd say about fifteen? Huh?" he asked.

I nodded.

"Well, fifteen will do mate. I got a bed in back and ya can come and go as ya please, but as soon as I feel as though you aren't pulling ya weight, ya gotta go. No questions or any bullocks about it mate. AND don't let yasself be seen!" he said, offering me the last bit of his sandwich.

There was a loud crashing noise from behind a large curtain where I assumed the people visiting the tavern sat. He grunted as he got himself up off the crates, grabbed a large block of wood and opened the curtain. As I stood looking out of the kitchen to the main seating area of the tavern, there stood red-haired Harold. Well, "stood" is a relative term, for he was drunk. His accent was even worse in his drunkenness.

"Reggie-- get ya fat black ass out hea and serve me a drink," he slurred.

"You know I told you and ya gang of Irish girls aren't allowed back in here," Raymond said, placing the wood block on his shoulder behind his neck.

As they exchanged shots back and forth, I slithered out the back door. My energy had been renewed and I was ready to do some hunting. I waited by the front of the alley until Harold finally was rolled out by Raymond, and I followed him. I would not be able to interrogate him out on the street because he was stronger than me. I needed something for leverage, such as a pet, or hopefully a child, and if I was really lucky, a wife. I followed him as he staggered down a long dusty road to his home. I smiled because there were little wooden toys outside of the home that looked like something I would play with as a youngster. This was what I needed. I just needed to get my timing correct for when I struck.

I was stronger now. I was even smarter now. I had the knowledge of strategy on my side now. This would not be as sloppy as the orphanage. I would do these with thought. Since Harold was the first one I found, he would do the honor of feeling my blade first. He and his son were just having a nice little father-son interaction by the time I reached the house. It was an awfully sweet time.

I watched his son go in and out of their house. I was surprised that he was so comfortable leaving the back room window open. I climbed into the bedroom and hid behind a chair in the main room. I waited until I heard the pitter-patter of little feet coming around the corner, and I grabbed the boy and put him in a chokehold before he could get a good scream out.

"Shhhhhh," I whispered in his ear.

His heart was racing. I could feel it pumping against my chest as I held him close to me. After his son didn't come back out, Harold crept around the corner, calling the little one's name. I stood there with his what appeared to be seven-year-old son with my arm wrapped around his throat and my knife at his eye. My cheek was directly pressed against his. Anytime the tike struggled, I tightened my arm around his little throat, cutting off his breath for a short time until he stilled himself.

"Hullo there, Harold. Just 'avin a litlo chat wiv ya boy 'ere," I said, looking Harold directly in his eyes.

"Ah well, if it innt litlo Finga Cutta. Seems as ya r' a tough one ya is," he said, sliding his way into the home.

"Don't make anotha move or ya litlo one here won't be able to see. See, I was askin 'im if he knew the otha guy who was witcha when ya killed me litlo bruva? He said he didn't know. Ya think ya can give him a hint?" I asked as his son lost oxygen again.

"Ya don't wanna be doin this roight now, kiddo. Weer strong now me boy. Ya moight not make it out of this house. Why don't ya just let me son go and you and me have it out, huh?" he says, stalling me.

This time, when I tightened my arm around his son's throat, I dragged the knife down his cheek. Poor lad couldn't squeal with my arm muscle in his throat. Harold began to come toward us. I stepped back to the wall and put the knife back on his son's eye.

"NAME!!" I shouted at him.

He jumped that time. He knew I was very serious at that point.

"McCreary-- 'is name is McCreary, just let me boy go," he sputtered through tears.

"Ya know I need to pay 'im a visit afta I leave 'ere now, don't cha? Where do I foind 'im?" I asked.

"Oh trust me, ya litlo shite, ya not makin it out ov 'ere. It's five houses up, green 'ouse onna left," he said with confidence.

"Neiver is ya son," I said, sliding the knife into his eye socket. I quickly snatched the knife out and dug the knife into his chest, sliding it twice into the same area between his two top ribs.

"NOOO!!!" Harold cried out.

He did exactly what I expected him to do: he rushed me. I dodged his first clumsy, blind swing and the knife slid through his ribcage, puncturing his lung. He lost all his fight at that point. There was a slight gush of warm air followed by blood splattering on my wrist. His breathing had a whistle to it. I pushed him off me and slid him up on the wall to where he was sitting up. I heard a commotion behind me. I rolled off him and hid behind a curtain. As I went behind the curtain, I held my bloody finger to my lips in a 'shushing' motion.

"Harold, ya left tha door open ya dolt," I heard a woman's voice say.

Harold was trying to warn her. He tried to speak, but the blood had already begun to fill his lungs at that point, and all he could do was sputter up redness and let it dribble down his chin. I peeked from the side of the curtain as she screamed and ran to her son. She dropped what food she had from the market.

"Andrew! What 'appended son? No, no, no, no, no, no!" she screamed as she hugged her son to her bosom.

I came up behind her and snatched her hair so that we met eyes right before I slit her throat. I laughed as her blood spewed on Harold's face. She wriggled a little while but eventually stopped. I watched the entire process. Harold kept pointing at her and I finally turned her over and saw she was pregnant. I looked at Harold as I slid the knife into her plump stomach three times. It took all the energy he had to close his eyes and look away. I walked over to Harold, grabbed his tangled and matted red hair, *and stabbed him in his throat. I poked him once more for good measure. He gurgled something I couldn't understand.*

I looked through the house until I found a place to wash myself. I took some of the food they had and ate, looking at the bodies as the lives drained from them. I walked to the back window that I had climbed through earlier. And he said I wouldn't make it out of there. I heard my mother laughing at me in my head. I walked out into the evening and began to count houses, looking for a green one, before I headed back to Ray's Tavern.

May 11, 1888

Today, the paper was ringing the alarm of what was found in Ms. Carlisle's home.

Jack the Ripper claims another victim!!
Scotland Yard to increase patrols at night.

I got back to the market and cackled madly at the article. The silly people are still calling them murders. I will not continue to allow this to bother me. They actually believe that increasing the patrols will cause me to stop. I am going to go back to the whores that I was killing before. They cannot say for sure what time Ms. Carlisle was painted, or killed as they like to call it. I'm not bothered by it. The Bobbies are saying that they have someone in mind and that they have leads. But, I know they are only saying this to put the minds of the readers at ease. They know and I know they have no leads. Sarah loves this. While I read the paper, she blew a kiss at me in the darkness of the back room.

Since my daytime attack, I've decided not to go out during the day again. They can find the bodies on the same day if I do it in the wee hours of the morning. I have the benefit of the shroud of night at those times. I'm not worried about the increased patrols.

By Friday night, I was looking for my next victim. I've moved away from the bars and taverns. I've just browsed the streets. I've seen one or two, but I let them be for one reason or another. There's no reason to rush. Somethings take time. Others don't. I'm not too bothered. I'm continuing to work in the market with no interruptions from anyone. I just invest in more paint brushes when I have the time. The itch is there.

I do not want anyone to feel as though I don't want to continue at this point. I am not bound by hatred for Sarah anymore; I just now want to see more of the reports in the paper. They make themselves look very daft with their reports. One report said that the Ripper is some sort of monster with sharp, ragged teeth and claws, attacking women at random. But they do not know that it takes time to choose who and where I will create my works of art.

They've said things about how Ms. Carlisle's brother died as well, in some part of America, but I know what killed him, a great steak and a side of mash. This makes me smile, because he was all she had left and thus no one to help her. She deserved what she got, because I couldn't get Ms. Applegum like I wanted. But, that's fine too. Sarah will make sure to explain to them what caused them to be where they were. Some "witnesses" feel as though a ghost killed these women or some sort of spiritual being that disliked what they were doing. I did chuckle at this one. But at any rate, I do see that hard work pays off. I know about that thanks to the man's name that I use now.

"Thomas, this ain't no library," Ben said as I was reading and thinking about it.

I was so lost in the paper that I did not realize that he had awaken and had been watching me for the past two minutes. I laughed because I knew he was only buggering about.

"Yeah, well it sure as hell doesn't feel like a butcher's shop when I haven't had to cut anything in a while," I laughed back to him.

If he had known how many cuts I made last Saturday, he would not be laughing with me. He just shook his head and returned to the back to get some paperwork done. I just need to consider my next move. I need to be careful. Even though I'm not named in anything, I feel as though eyes are on me. Sarah will make sure to inform me of any type of outside threats that may try and stop me from doing what I need to. I know that I will be back out in the dark looking for victims. I do not have a problem with it. Stalking is now my specialty.

October 01, 1867

I found the green house without a problem. The homes were all spread apart down a wide dirt road. I picked the lock in the cellar window. I loved windows because I was just small enough to fit in and smart enough to pick almost any lock. I slinked into the dark area and waited quietly for a few hours to get accustomed to what I saw. It was night finally. I just listened. I was behind the steps, shaded perfectly.

My eyes had just begun to adjust to the darkness when I heard the lock up the stairs fumble open. They were using the cellar to store things that they had stolen from people. I could barely contain my anger thinking about what they had stolen from the Wilschire's. Two men came in and I was sure that one of them was McCreary. He came down the stairs first, by himself. I saw his red hair before the door closed and another man came down to where I could only see his boots.

"Went down to get Harold an' him and 'is family are dead, mate. It's pretty bad too. They even stabbed the baby she was carryin. It's pretty bad, man," the unknown man said in his funny accent.

I couldn't help but smile behind it.

"Fokin' shite. Me brova. I know who did this. Those fokin spics wanna war, we'll give 'em more war than they will ever be able to handle," McCreary said back to him.

I pulled my knife out as they walked up the steps chattering about what the next plan was and getting the rest of the guys together. Unfortunately, he did not realize his plans would be placed on the back burner when he found out who was doing this to them. I could not wait. But I needed to. The funny thing about being whatever it was they claimed they were, they wouldn't know who had attacked them. I had the element of surprise, so it would be wonderful. I didn't feel like I had a sickness or some sort of disease. I felt as though they were the sickness or the disease. So, I waited. I waited until I heard the men come in and argue about what happened to their fallen brother. They had no idea what losing a brother was like. They had no care or feeling for anyone. They had no clue who or what had done such a horrible thing to Harold.

After about forty-five minutes of arguing, the upstairs became silent. Then, I heard a woman sending someone to bed and things of that nature.

169

I crept from behind the stairway and looked around the cellar for something other than the little knife I had. It was small and slender and it was the knife that Thomas gave me. So, I felt it was good for exacting my revenge, and I was hungry for it. I did find a couple things that I was looking for. I placed them by the top of the steps so that I could take time to silently pick the lock.

Opening the door, the home was large. There was another set of stairs that no doubt led up to his lovely family. I looked over to the mantle and saw an empty shelf for a rifle. I heard someone clear his throat and spit. I peeked around the door and saw the booted man at the door with his back to the home. He was sure that whoever had done this to Harold would come to the front door. How silly of him. There was a large sitting area with different furniture spread all around. I slowly crept around the two small chairs.

As I waited, I heard him snoring, so I knew I was doing fine. I had no idea what time it was. While his back was leaned against the outside door frame, I slowly leaned toward him and waited until I was sure he was asleep. I dug my knife into his throat. He made a few gagging noises, but they weren't loud enough to get anyone's attention upstairs. I turned toward the steps and made my way upstairs slowly. As soon as I would hear a creaking noise, I would skip that step.

After reaching the top of the steps, I looked around and saw three rooms-- two on the left and one on the right in the center. I crept up to the one on the right. I peeked in, saw a large bed, and assumed it was the main room where McCreary and the woman slept. I crept to each of the other rooms and saw a boy and a girl in the first and second, respectively. Surprisingly, the children were asleep as well. I was sure that they would be wide awake.

I went back downstairs, checking for any new entries, and got a nice heavy piece of wood from near the fireplace. Since it was nowhere near wintertime, there was plenty of wood to use. I grabbed the other utensils I had from the cellar and walked back upstairs. I slid back into the wife's room and pushed the bed to wake her. As soon as she sat up, I used the wooden block on her head and knocked her out instantly. The two children put up no fight. Within minutes, I had them all bound and gagged at the top of the steps in a nice little circle facing outwards from each other. I managed to find a third item that would assist me with making this all come together. The first item I had taken from the cellar was twine and the second was a nice, full lantern of oil that was surely taken from the Wilschire farm.

When I removed the top of the lantern and began to pour the thick oil on the three of them, the woman awoke and began to mumble loudly. I made sure she was nice and saturated with the oil. I then poured a nice amount on her two young ones. I used twice the amount of twine on mom just to make sure she was not able to escape. I got the wood piece and headed back downstairs. I stood at the foot of the stairs so that I could watch mom and the kiddies, yet be close enough to the door to surprise my foe. I could tell the lot of them weren't that smart. That was really all the advantage that I needed.

A few moments later, I saw the youngest wriggling in the darkness. I quickly went over to her, looked her in the eyes, and opened up her stomach with my knife. I did not need any distractions at this point and I wanted to keep her alive for the grand finale. Her eyes fluttered a little, but she was alive. She leaned her head onto her mother's shoulder. It looked as though they were posing for a picture. This made me laugh. I continued to sit on the foot of the stairs until I heard shuffling outside the main door.

"Lucky, wake ya bloomin' arse up! Ya always…sleepin…onna…Fokin shite, mate, who did this to ya?" I heard McCreary say.

"Oh no, Martha? Martha my love? Say something!" I waited until I heard his voice come closer to the door.

As soon as I saw his left knee enter into the door, I swung the wood as hard as my arms allowed me to. Unlike Betty's feeble attempt, mine found its target. There was a satisfying CRACK sound as his knee shattered. He fell face-first into the home, sending his rifle under one of the sitting room chairs. I brought the wood block down onto his left hand with even more force and this made his hand explode like a beaten cherry filled sack. His hand was useless now, but he was quick enough to get onto his back and jab me in the privates with his right hand. This sent me to the bottom step behind me. It was not a problem because I needed him upstairs anyway.

"Whateva ya've done to me family, Finga Cutta, I'm gonna do worse to ya," he threatened me.

I was still silent as I scurried backwards up the stairs. I tried to give him a look of fear and pain as he scrambled to his feet. Good job, little rabbit. He was in no condition to climb any stairs. He limped up after me. I got close to the top step and jumped up, reaching into my pocket for the third item, a lovely book of matches. As he reached the top of the stairs, I lit a match and looked at him as I dropped it onto his wriggling wife. The oil instantly caught and burned slowly through her mouth gag, allowing her to scream. McCreary fell to the floor and I seized the opportunity. I ran through the spreading fire and connected my knee to his face while he began sobbing. My groin was still aching from his punch, but I found my target. His head snapped back, hitting the wall behind him and sending him into a daze. I climbed on top of his back so that I could get close to his ear. I grabbed a handful of his hair, pulled my knife from my pocket, and propped his chin on the base of the sharp utensil. It dug into his skin, causing little red droplets to form on my thumbnail. The twine that bound his family was made from metal, so it would not give when the fire spread to his little ones, engulfing their bodies as well.

"Wotch 'em, McCreary. Wotch 'em loike I hadda wotch me lilto bruva bleed to def loike a gutted piggy. I'm gonna foind Manny and do tha same fing to 'im," I whispered in his ear.

I watched as their skin turned into black charcoaled putty on their faces and their struggling came to an end. McCreary struggled a few times and I had to eventually stab him in his right hand to make him stop. I began to hear a commotion outside behind me.

"Nighty-night, McCreary. Tis a shame we don't have more time together; I would give ya the same treatment ya gave Jake, ya bastard," I said to him, slitting his throat.

I climbed off McCreary, stumbled down the steps, and kicked the door shut. I then ran and locked the door and placed the large piece of wood in between the door and the wall beside it. I ran back upstairs; there were two more lanterns on each side of the upstairs walls and I grabbed both of them. I covered McCreary who was close to the fire and made a trail back down the stairs. I couldn't have anyone else from his lot seeing me. I lit the trail that I left as someone broke the door in, but I was already in the cellar heading to the window. I hung around a bit to make sure that no one made it out alive. After all, they thought that they had burned me alive. In all my rage, I had forgotten to ask McCreary about Manny and his whereabouts. At this point, I assumed that Manny was the one whose finger I had cut off. I'm sure that he was outside cutting into Jake that fateful day. Finding him was the next thing on my list.

May 20, 1888

Since Ms. Carlisle, I've been spending more and more time at the cottage. You see, here I have more time to think. I can actually put together better ideas this way. I know that for Sarah, it is all about the artwork. Sarah does not just want any type of kill. She needs a public visual of the dead victims, something that everyone will see. To top it off, the stupid Scotland Yard bobbies giving me the "Jack the Ripper" namesake is something even I did not expect. I thought that maybe if I kept things quiet for a while, the Jack the Ripper story would die down. But, every day that I walk past the paper, there is a new story about the silly name they've given me.

People are coming out pretending to be Jack the Ripper almost every day now. The bobbies are more overwhelmed with pursuing false impersonators than trying to find the actual culprit. One man came dressed to the tee in an over-exaggerated outfit, with knives and all, into the Scotland Yard station. They even had a woman come in and say she was the killer. I would read and laugh for hours while all this was going on. But, this is really no laughing matter. It upsets me because I am actually out and about trying to find these proper art pieces and these falsehoods are trying to take credit for it. I'm thinking about going down to Scotland Yard and killing these fakes myself.

On top of that, Sarah is becoming impatient again. She hasn't started to bother my dreams yet. But, if she does, it won't be a problem. I know what I want to do. This next one will be something they will write about for years to come. Even though there are increased patrols and things, the Scotland Yard department cannot be everywhere. This is where my patience is really being tested. Nonetheless, any other kills that I may paint out at this cottage mean nothing to her.

What I've started doing during my lunch hour is to go out to look for different hiding spots. These spots aren't just for me; I will hide my tools there as well. I have chosen three spots that are not travelled often. I have to go to each area twice a day. Once during the day at lunch hour and another time at night. During the daytime, I want to see how many people are around these areas.

After surveying these places and inserting my knives and utensils in different hidden areas, all I have to do is wait. The nights are not as eventful as I would like them to be. The women aren't out and about as they usually are. Mainly because the new, nightly constable patrols make it difficult for them to make their coin. I have no problem actually looking for the women I want to kill, but I do need to avoid the view of the constables. I know that I can outsmart them still.

For at least two weeks, I could not find the perfect art piece that I was looking for. I was stopped a few times and had to give the constables false information. It was very simple to make up some sort of lie or name. I am an average looking male with a typical height and stature. I continue to shave myself so I have nothing identifiable on my person. It is very simple to avoid too many of them with my black cloak and hat on, or by simply going inside a building.

To have the time I need to complete the artistry is my issue. I can get one of the whores walking up and down the road, but I will not be able to do anything with them. I can watch people and they will not see me at all. A few paintings walk past, but I don't want to strike too fast. Timing is of the utmost importance in this situation. This isn't the longest I've had to wait for a good kill.

April 05, 1870

It took me two and a half years to find any trace of Manny. After I took care of the McCreary's, I went to different houses looking for food and warmth. I came across a shelter for boys, but I left the first night because I was afraid of another Happy Sunshine incident. After reading in the paper that the previous murders that I had committed were blamed on rival gang members, I knew I was on the right track. I figured a twelve-year-old child was hard to discern as a murderer.

I stayed in the same area where I had killed the three people on Manny's team. At this point, my rage was at an all-time high. I could not find him, and it was not enough to have just missed him or read about how he had tried to recruit more people to his side. I found out that there were foreign areas that different travelers would stay for a time. I finally found the Irish village. It was like a town inside of a town. At the age of eighteen, I did not understand as much as I do now. You would have people from Spain or Germany dwelling in their own communities.

But at any rate, I found Manny's little Irish area. As I searched around, I found out he had no family. That was fine. He would be enough. At my age, I was in prime shape and had grown taller than a normal eighteen-year-old. I was constantly doing press ups while thinking of what I would do to him. I had begun to follow him at times. I would need to break away if it had gotten too dangerous. For instance, it may have been me and his new group on a long, dark road, and it would be too difficult to not be seen. Even with my height at the time, he was still a little taller than I was. But, my anger had made me taller than he was, in my mind.

One night, I finally followed him to his home. I sat outside for hours, watching to see what he was doing, who he had over, and what time he slept, and I judged that by what time all the lanterns were put out. I did this for several days. I thought about what I would do to him for some time. I waited until he left one day, picked his lock, and entered his home. I needed to learn his home like the back of my hand. It was nothing huge. It was a long, one-bedroom home with a large main room. There weren't many hiding spaces, so I needed to know what and where everything was. This didn't take long. I was able to remember everything I needed.

While in the only bedroom one morning, I heard keys jingling at the lock of the front door. I had no choice because he would have seen me if I ran out. So, I hid under the bed as silently as possible. This was early in the morning and I could tell he was already drunk because had slurred speech. He stumbled through the hallway past his sleeping quarters and went directly to the lavatory. I slid my knife from my pants ever so gently. He stumbled back past his door as I watched his feet from below the bed.

"Fook all ya Bastids!" he shouted, slamming the front door of the home.

He fumbled back into the room and sat on the edge of the bed closest to the door. He removed his shoes and laid back on the bed. I scurried over to make sure I was away from where the arch in the bed formed. It took little time before he began to snore. I slid from underneath the bed and crept around to where he laid. With a crouch and quick jump, I landed directly on his chest and one arm. Before he could react, I stabbed the armpit of his free arm and covered his mouth with my free hand.

" 'Ello Manny, me boy. It's ya good ole pal, FingaCutta. Tell McCreary and Harold I said 'Hi' wouldja?" I said in a voice I did not recognize as my own.

I gashed my knife into his throat until I heard the tip of the knife hit the bone in the back of his neck. Blood erupted from the wound and came through my fingers over his mouth. The red spurted from his throat and all over my grinning face and hair. I felt it hit my eyes but I could not and would not blink. For I could not miss a moment of this. This was epic to me. I would laugh for days into my adulthood thinking of how I exacted my revenge on Manny and his band of wildlings. He bucked as a horse and it reminded me of the times on the farm where I would help Thomas break in new ones. He wanted to escape. I could feel his hand behind me squirming and clawing at my back as I slashed his throat again and again. I thought that the more I slashed, the more blood I would taste. I did not realize that I was shrieking with laughter. Then, I thought of Jake and how he would not be able to see this. I began to cry and laugh at the same time.

"Why did you take him from me!?" I yelled in his face as he gurgled and choked on his own blood.

I stabbed until I nearly decapitated him. He had been long dead since I started shouting. I was heaving now. My breathing was almost labored, but I needed to leave. I ripped off my bloody shirt, went into the bath, and washed my face and hands as cleanly as I could and crept out into the afternoon. I closed and locked the door and left the little Irish sub town. I walked. I knew the top of my pants had blood on them but I had tied my shirt around it to cover that. After I had gotten almost two miles away, I sat in an alley, vomited, and wept. I cried for Jake, Thomas and even that bitch Betty. I hoped they had seen this.

It was at this point that I rebirthed my promise to Jake not to kill anymore. That was, until I met Sarah.

May 21, 1888

JACK THE RIPPER FINALLY CAUGHT!!

I read the paper this morning. I couldn't believe my eyes. Now, I am thoroughly upset. There is nothing that Sarah can do to appease my feelings. They have made some silly arrest behind something that someone said about a man who someone saw out and about. Now, the authorities will not kill him soon. He has time to prove himself innocent. I may actually be able to assist him with his innocence.

Soon, I will be able to take a victim and not have any issue for the man caught. Just reading the in between the lines of the paper, I was able to assess that there will not be as many patrols out at night as there have been lately. Something about too much money was being spent on overtime for the bobbies. That's not important. I will wait some time to make sure that what I am assuming is true. I can just go out tonight and take a life because these silly women will be right back out since they feel very safe now. The monster that they call 'Jack' is finally off the streets.

I smile at this because I am nowhere near off the streets; they aren't as safe as they would like to think. Sarah runs her fingers over my mind. Something needs to be done and soon. My itch has been reawakened with Ms. Carlisle, the widow. I wonder if she is with her dead husband now or if she is burning in hell for her mistreatment of the little ones. But, that's not important; my next painting is. As I said earlier, I will make this one important. It will be seen. It has to be seen.

May 24, 1888

A few days after finding out "Jack" had been caught, we began to actually deliver meats to people. This has assisted me with learning more about London. I have been able to further stretch the locations of my paintings. I have increased from three to eight spots where I am able to keep items for my next picture.

I feel sad when I walk past Tabitha's home on certain occasions. I wonder what is happening to her garden, where her plants are undoubtedly overgrown with weeds and things. She will not be able to fix that beautiful area. It's now covered in black weeds and vines that Sarah has made grow there. Right from Baggins' moldy mouth. But, I forget as soon as I pass by. Sarah changes my mind in some way or another. For some reason, I'm not as bitter as I was a few weeks ago. I think Ms. Carlisle was a filter for my bitterness. I really do not know.

At any rate, the other night I crept to my new area of hidden tools. I have accumulated so many from my different travels. I have even gone to the cottage and taken most of them that I've stored there and spread them throughout London.

I got myself hidden into one of my spots and waited. There were nearly no bobbies out and about this night. I knew I had to commit a murder very soon to avoid the wrong person taking credit for my artworks. I was in a bad part of town. So, I had to make this one very special. I finally found a target and Sarah agreed with my selection. As she came around the corner huffing about something or other, I snatched her like a spider with a fresh fly in its web. I slammed her into a wall and then again to the ground. I worked fast so as to get as much wind out of her as possible. My gloves almost made her slip from my strong grip.

When she hit the ground, I punched her in the stomach just to be sure. I dragged her further into the alley. More like in the middle. I then turned her on to her belly, lifted her right arm and drove my knee into the back of her elbow, breaking her arm. She wanted to scream but had no air to do so. I snatched my knife from my hidden stash spot and serrated her vocal chords and trachea in the same moment. I took her left arm and performed the same act as I did to the right. The popping noise it made was beyond satisfying. The puddle of blood forming in front of her as she jerked up and down into it was splashing droplets on my pants. I snickered because they would be burned soon enough. As the last bit of life left her, I slit her ears off and pocketed them. I was reaching down to turn her over when from behind me I heard:

"Oi!! What's goin' on ova thea?" a man's voice yells down the alley.

I froze for a moment. The haze that Sarah had over me was leaving. The same wooziness I was feeling when I stabbed my knife into Tabitha's brain was what was leaving me now. I became rational then. I was now aware of my surroundings and seeing things for what they were. I was a monster and I didn't want anyone to see me.

I was sure that I checked the area to make sure there was no one near. I stayed there and crouched over her. My long coat was beginning to soak some of the water and blood mixture into its fabric. I had no clue how much he may have seen. I looked forward to the opening at the other end of the alley. I did not want to turn around, for I did not want him to possibly see my face. I had a smaller shoe size on and my feet were already aching. I could hear his feet shuffle closer to me. He may have been drunk because his walk was stumbled. When I felt that he was about ten paces away from me, I stood and darted off.

"Hey!" he yelled.

He tried to take chase and I heard him fall over something.

"Oh my God!" I heard him exclaim as I made it to the mouth of the alley.

Exiting the alley was slightly difficult, for I did not want to attract any attention. It wasn't late enough for the streets to be empty, and I did not want to take any chances if there were a lot out. As I left, I began to run through different alleys and walked the streets where there weren't any alleys to run in. I did this until I was at least a mile away from the area. It took me slightly longer to get home, but it was worth it. Before I would go into an alley, I would examine my surroundings very carefully to make sure no one was around. Upon arriving home, I did the normal routine of washing and burning everything. This was difficult because it took time for me time to catch my breath. Now, all I could do was wait.

It took two days before there was anything worth reading about me in the paper. It is now funny that I actually consider myself the murderer they are describing in the paper. "Jack the Ripper," as they have it written in the paper. At any rate, I stopped by recently and obtained the morning paper and read in large bold print:

Wrongfully Accused Released!
Jack the Ripper Still at Large!

In the paper, the daft reporters stated that an eyewitness saw a large man brutally defiling a young woman. Ha! I never defiled these horrible leeches of a species. They weren't worth my erection. But this is what I want. I want no one to take credit for what I painted. Don't get me wrong, I do not care whether or not the man is hanged. I just don't want him to take the credit for what I have done.

I am beginning feel that I may need to turn myself in. I am starting to wonder that I may just be wrong. Maybe I am being too harsh with my punishment of these women, all behind what Betty did? No. I wasn't too harsh. She killed my brother as though she herself had done it with her own hands. In the shop this morning, I watched as Sarah looked at herself in the reflection in the glass of the meat section. I have also started to realize that she has shown herself to me in her ghastly form less and less. I don't know what meaning this has on my actions, but I have just noticed it today. It was really her who opened the door to this spree that I am having. She seems to be having a good time now. And loving every bit of this. She will not allow me to turn myself in. She would find a way to make me kill myself before I would to do such a thing. I think about Sarah and how silly my mind was about her. And actually, to this point in my life, it still is.

After Manny, I had no other anger or desire to kill anyone. I was pleased with the way his body had shivered its last shakes after my knife penetrated his throat. I left Ray's Tavern and began my path of becoming a successful adult and working my way through life. During that time, I obtained all manner of jobs, from paperboy to stock boy to waiter. But up until about two years ago, I was a delivery boy.

This was where I met her. Sarah. She was the most beautiful woman I had ever seen. Even more beautiful than Betty. I was no longer an angry and hurt teenager, but a full-grown man who had manly desires. I delivered a package on her street early one morning and she came out to the door wearing something that was not all together ladylike, but it was still subtle enough to be decent. It was a long evening gown with barely a hint of her nipple showing. Her hair fell down her back in red tendrils and was all together wonderful. She had the greenest of eyes and they had a brown cherry outside to them. Her nose was a center of perfection on her face. I could see that her nightgown had bunched up around her nether regions and shown a small amount of hair that was the same color as her head. Her voice was a symphony of exquisiteness. I had never believed in love at first site, but this was it.

" 'Ello, koind sir. 'Ow are ya?" she had asked as she accepted her package.

I was at a total loss for words the first time she came to the door. I fell bloody silent as soon as I saw her. I could not find anything to say, so I just stood there with my mouth open. I was taken aback by her beauty. My words were unable to be found. She smiled at me. She knew how beautiful she was, and how beautiful I found her. She hummed whatever tune was in her head, turned away and closed the door.

"Hi," I whispered to no one.

She was a red headed angel to me. I could not contain myself. I stalked her. I knew that I had to be going insane. This woman, who did not even know my name, had me enthralled. I moved up the street, several doors down from her, and I could not keep myself away from her home. I had her schedule down to the second. Every week she would start by going to the market then cleaning her home. I spent too much time looking in her window while she bathed.

Then, my love for her began to grow to hate as I began to see different men come in and out of her bed. They were using her and she allowed this to happen. I snuck into her home from time to time and stole the panties that she had not washed. I would masturbate on them and sneak them

184

back into her home. I don't know why it gave me a rush to see them hanging from the line where she dried her clothes.

I became obsessed with her. There were many nights that I sat underneath her window while she would sing and dance in her bedroom. She did not know that my infatuation had become a rage. One night, while some random man met her in her bedroom, I snuck in and stole a pair of her panties. They were soiled with a mixture of her woman juices, and I smelled a man on them as well. I did the smelling at home and I burned them. I didn't masturbate in them as I normally did. I was infuriated. That was the day that I had marched back over to her home and heard her calling out Edgar's name. She had to be taught not to play with my emotions in this manner. She was so involved with obtaining whatever coin he would give her that she had not heard me downstairs fumbling quietly through her kitchen utensils looking for the proper weapon of choice.

As I heard the creaking of the bed, I looked to the stairs and knew that she would pay for these transgressions. I snickered. My mother's voice was constantly egging me on to complete the task. I took each step carefully and edged my way upstairs. Their sexual romp was so loud she could not even hear the creaking that the door made as I entered. By the time she saw me, the knife I had was already buried in good ole Edgars back. He tried to turn over, but my grip was strong and the knife was in my hand. She looked at me with those green eyes in utter shock and surprise. The knife went deep into her chest. She reached up and swiped at my face, scratching me beneath my left eye. But I was laughing.

Edgar got one good punch in my cheek as the blood trailed down his face. He was on his knees in the bed and wasn't able to really put as much energy into it as he wanted. I had stabbed him clean in the face. I did not realize that I had gotten his eye at that time, but it did the trick. I swiped

185

quickly at his neck, gashing him as he fell backwards. Sarah heaved a few
more times and that was all there was left of her. I felt tears forming on my
face as I went into the bath and cut on the hot water in her basin. I sat on
the floor sobbing for a moment, stood up, and felt the hot water going cold.
I then took the trek down to the basement of her home to light the furnace
again. After finishing Edgar off, I went home and began to pack my things.
There was no need for me to stay on this accursed street anymore. I left in
the darkness of the night. I had my rent paid up for the time that I had
stayed and informed the owner through a letter that I had found another
position and would be moving closer to it. The next week or so, I found
Mr. Vanschlatt. I had no one else at that point. For some reason, my
mother stopped speaking to me again for some time.

June 03, 1888

With the release of the man who would have been me, I don't want
another killing right now. So, I've actually begun to think about moving
from London. I don't know where I want to go. I do know that I want to
leave here. There is too much pain and too many memories that have
had negative effects on my life here. I have to get out of here, and I don't
have a clue of how to do so. When I ask if there is any way I can work
more hours, Ben shakes his head and talks about how new businesses are
taking money from him and how he won't really be able to support such
a thing. I only pay about two shillings for my room now and cannot
afford to put aside money for anything else. I feel stuck. But, I cannot
allow that to hinder me from my next piece of art. I will do maybe a few
more here and then take my gallery on the road. Then I will go from
showing London what I can do to showing the world. I don't know or
care if Sarah approves of this.

"I didn't want to kill after Manny," I whispered recently in the store.

" 'Avin a chat wif yasself, mate?" Ben asked.

"Oh yes, I am. I am sorry; I was off in my own world. Would you mind if I took the rest of the day off, Ben? I don't think I am feeling to well for work," I asked.

"Oi, of course man. Just clean what you buggered up and head on out. I got it from here," he replied.

"Not a problem. Thanks," I said, removing my apron.

"Daft mate, you never ask for time off. I feel like you are some sorta' machine or sumfin. Go on, be off with ya," he said.

I laughed and headed to the back of the cutting room. I don't think he noticed or cared that some of the carving utensils had come up missing. Ben made enough money to buy as many as he needed to.

That night, I went back to plotting out my next victim. I could not be in the same area because, of course, there were bobbies out and about now. Not as many as last time, but still they were there. So, I went into taverns and waited until it was a good hour to go and muddle about. I still did not feel as though there was anything that I could do to really make the killing a public thing.

That was when it came to me. I was leaving one of the eight hidden areas that I had and saw the manhole cover. I had completely forgotten about the sewer that I had done so much research on when I was thinking about killing Tabitha and how she would look laid on the ground with the blood running from her body. I knew then that I would take one down there. I just needed to get some things together so that it would be easy for the selected woman's demise. Just to make sure, I took time after work over the next few days to make sure that the night shift had not changed. It was a little difficult to go down into the sewer system with all the constables about, but I was able to creep in unseen.

The next few days, I was at the cottage getting my tools together. I needed wood and wheels. They were both easy to obtain from work. We had palettes that weren't used completely and would be thrown away. That was the wood. I just went around to a toy store and obtained an actual wagon to remove the wheels. The only real issue I had was being able to build the whole thing in the sewer near the area where I would create the artwork. This took some time because after I broke down the palette, I would need to take the wood to the area piece by piece, and that was somewhat difficult. I did it by wrapping them in a sheet. Had I not been in shape, this would have been really difficult. I was able to get a good five to six board pieces in and all four wheels.

Two nights later, I nailed them together to make a crude wagon with a long rope to drag it around. Standing it up against a wall was not hard and it would easily be mistaken for trash. After that was completed, I went to get some candles. I have no idea why I wanted these. I don't even think that it was I who wanted them, but Sarah. She was very enthusiastic about them for some reason. When I went to the market to look for food, she floated over and around the candles telling me we needed them for the next woman that I would get.

Eight. I don't know why it was eight exactly, but that was what she wanted. I just laughed and made the purchase. Sarah has begun to seem more involved with the murders than normal. I can't be concerned about that at this point. I went home and set up the candles to see what they would look like and if she liked the setup for the artwork.

Sarah and I came to an agreement that this will be the last murder that I will commit in London. I will take the ferry to America and continue my paintings. I'm sure that there are harlots and jezebels that need to be exposed there as well. I will take a satchel of all of my items and keep them hidden with my wagon for the coup de grace that I have planned. The next night, I made sure to soak my glove in the chloroform. I would use the same tactic I used with Rose. So, I went back out on another night. I waited for hours and there was nothing. I'll try again tomorrow.

June 12, 1888

It took me three nights before I lucked up on tonight's painting. She was wearing a short, red, flared dress, a short-sleeved grey shirt, and long, black fishnet stockings. As I grabbed her and pulled her close to me, I could smell the sick smell of her and a random man's sweat on her body. I almost erupted in laughter as she bit down on my inner finger, and the bite began to pain me less and less as she lost all of her motor skills. Some may call me crazy, but I chuckled at this as I walked toward the mouth of the alleyway to try and get to my destination. I am not crazy or an insane man. I have complete control over my senses and I do not do the same thing over and over again expecting a different outcome. But, I could have laughed at this all night. I checked again to see if anyone was coming and quickly removed the cover to the underground waterway. The sewage smell instantly engulfed my nostrils and I gagged somewhat at the smell. I am still surprised that something such as this will turn my gullet.

I wrapped up the still breathing young lady in a nice blanket and some twine. I took the time to make sure her mouth was covered, just in case she mysteriously woke up. As I slung her body through the opening, I looked again to make sure there was no one around and covered the entrance again. When I got into the cold, dank, wetness, my mind suddenly went back to Tabitha, the amazing nights that we had, and how before, I wanted this to be her. I can almost smile at this now.

But at any rate, I shuffled the small wagon from the hidden area and got her body on it ever so carefully. The dripping noises that I heard in the stoned underground keep were very loud against the background silence and the creaking, wobbling cart. I took care not to bruise the painting any more than I already had trying to get her down there. She sustained a broken leg; I only noticed this due to the cracking noise her leg made as I placed it on the sturdy, self-made wagon. For every possible corner that I got to in the underground tunnels, I parked the wagon in the shadows and made a quick check for anyone. Sarah assured me that no one was around, but for some reason I did not trust her tonight. She seemed extremely docile and very all-together. She was too calm and I felt a sort of uneasiness. It was fine though, because we would both leave after tonight. For some reason, whenever I thought about this, she would always cackle as though she knew something I did not about our departure.

I trekked on to our destination. In the process, the chloroform had to have worn off, because when we arrived, the painting's eyes were wide and darting around our location. The mumbles from under her mouth gag, which I made with her own soiled panties, were barely heard. We finally made it to the circle of the sewage area, all three of us. Sarah was facing me in the upper corner of the dim room. As I laid the art piece in the center of the circle, her eyes seemed to be trained on Sarah. I took a quick peek over my shoulder and Sarah was there. I looked back down at the whore and she looked back at me with her eyes the size of goose eggs.

"You see her? You see my Queen of Death?" I whispered to her. My voice shook like a mad man. Believe me, I am not mad.

She nodded her head up and down and looked back at Sarah with nothing but utter terror on her face. She began to have strings of liquid run from the corners of her eyes. It seemed as though she realized now the danger she was always in while she slinked up and down the streets at night looking for coin. I could feel my penis ready to burst from my pants from the excitement. I reached into my satchel and pulled out my sharp, shiny blade.

"I have saved and sharpened this one for days and weeks. It's the one my dad gave me. You should feel as happy as I am. I will be cleaning you of all the dirty, dirty deeds you have done, and make a beautiful piece of art that everyone will see. All at the same time," I laughed quietly in her ear.

Sarah made a loud hissing noise that made both me and the sweating, shaking woman on the cool ground jump. I remembered the candles before she could even point to them. I reached into the bag, took out the eight candles, and placed them in the areas that she wanted, in a crude sort of circle around the future dead woman. I lit each one as she asked. I then went back to the shivering woman, straddling her chest. She tried to turn over, but I pinned her shoulder to the ground.

I did not know exactly where I wanted to make my cuts. I was shaking myself now. I was so excited from the flickering lights of the candles and how Sarah was dancing around us, floating over them. It seemed as though the flames flickered from her dress, but that couldn't be. She was not actually there physically, so I must have been losing what was left of my mind. I cut the woman's shirt, exposing her chest and small breasts. Her chest heaved up and down as I slowly sliced across her nipple. Her eyes rolled into the back of her head from the pain for a second before they squinted shut. I smiled as she lurched up to my tightened testicles.

"I know, it will only hurt for a little while, I pr-promise," I stuttered out as I sliced across her other exposed nipple.

The knife was very sharp and made the cuts very easily. She was kicking and trying to scream now. Sarah wanted it more than ever, and I could tell by the way her hands graced my shoulders. I darted my free hand out, grasped the top of her forehead, and sliced her nose off in a clean swipe. I think she then fainted. I did the rest by slicing into her throat as blood flew over my face. I have grown used to the rusty smell, but the salty taste made me leave the knife where it ended in her flesh and stand up. I wiped my face quickly and vomited right there.

Sarah was nowhere to be seen. Then suddenly, there was a small, purple light forming over the painting. It let out a large aura that blew out all eight of the candles at once. Then, each of the candles lit up with a purple light, but within each light was the face of one of the paintings. Each woman who I had murdered in the London area was in each purple flickering flame. I did not want to see this, so I stepped out of the circle. I toppled one of the candles and it did not go out; the flame stayed lit. I even realized that when the flame touched my slacks, the flames caught on them and caused a cold fire that didn't really burn, but it felt like it was burning.

They were all looking at me. I wanted to scream. Even Tabitha was there, with that hateful eye. They were laughing at me. I wanted to run, and without looking, I stumbled over the cart, twisting my ankle in the process. Based upon the popping sound it made, it may have been broken. I was now facing the circle again and I was forced to see what happened next.

The light in the center flared out again, and this time it stayed open for a time. Out stepped Sarah. The laughing was now silenced, and Sarah looked at me, smiling. I found the energy to stand and I was a few feet away from her, but not close enough to touch her. I could smell the scent of her body, as she smelled the day she did when she was butchered by me. She laughed and scratched her head violently.

As she scratched, to my horror, blood began to squirt from her scalp and dribble down her face, arms and body. The blood looked like it was flowing from her head like a river, covering her arms, body and clothing. She began to tear bits of flesh from her skull. But she continued to scratch and rip, now with both hands. My stomach turned when I realized that she was not hiding an actual skull underneath, but something else. I began to shuffle away from this horrific bloodletting. And the blood was a black, sick, smelling liquid.

What I was seeing as Sarah ripped her own face from her body was blond hair and another face that I instantly recognized, and I shrieked in terror. I turned and shuffled away up the alleys and made it up the slippery ladder and out of the sewage area. I could hear her in my head the whole time. She whispered to me the things that I didn't want to hear. Sarah was just a pawn; now I see. Just a face to keep me to continue to do her bidding. I got to a corner of the road and crashed into a man.

"Oi, watch it there, ya drunk!" he yells, shaking me.

"My mother.." I said, leaning on the man as though I was drunk. I was only out of breath.

"Go on!" he yelled, pushing me to the ground. I looked up and began to see the purple aura coming from the alley.

I must have had it over my face that I was no longer looking at him. I stood up and could now run, ignoring the pain. I looked over my shoulder and saw that as the light passed the man, it wrapped around him and it almost overtook him.

I know it sounds very crazy as I write this now. But the man shook and began to point at me and run after me. When the light overtook him, he pointed at me.

"Time for bed, son. Be a good lad and give mum a kiss," he said.

I quickened my pace. There was no such thing as pain at this point. I slowed down a few times and continued my stride until I made it home. I am here now writing this because I know now and realize why Sarah-- well, Andrea-- knew; she knew this would be my last night in London for this reason. She has planned this the whole time. I even now hear her scratching at my bedroom door. I came here to warn everyo

June 15, 1888

I have no real reason or explanation of what or why I am compelled to begin recording what I am recording now. My name in London is Daniel Ratcliff. I am a bobby of Scotland Yard, Class of Seventeen. I was ranked third in my class of thirteen. That isn't important, but what I have to say is. I worked under Constable Blacksmith. His first name isn't important.

We had been working the "Jack the Ripper" murders and had not come across a single possible lead. Blacksmith would say that he always suspected Wilschire of being the murderer, but he never voiced it. I can believe him now, but it is no matter. When the owner of Ben's Butchers sent a letter today informing us that he had not heard from his best worker in the past few days and that he was worried, we went to his home.

We entered Wilschire's home after three knocks and called out with no response. Mr. Vanschlatt provided us with a key and no one was there. His home had been locked from the inside, and as we went to his resting quarters, his door was locked the same way. That door had no key, so Blacksmith and I had to break it in. We looked around and Blacksmith instantly found the journal. We told Vanschlatt that he could not allow anyone else into the room and that he would be held accountable for it if he or someone did before we could get another bobby down here to watch the door.

We sat in Blacksmith's office that entire evening reading this blasted thing. We took turns reading it aloud as one would get up to get tea and smoke a quick fag outside when everyone was gone. While he was gone, I began to hear small voices, but I did not believe it. Now, I am beginning to think that these voices are actually pushing me to write down what I am feeling and hearing.

"Ready to go on?" Blacksmith came in recently and erased the voices from my mind like cobwebs.

"Yeah, let's go on." I replied.

"What's on you, Ratcliff? You good to go on? As a matter of fact, go on and take off. I will wait until tomorrow to finish this. Seems as though you are as worse for wear as I am," he said.

"Understood, sir," I replied.

We ended our day and left Scotland Yard. He then grabbed my shoulder as we broke from each other and softly spun me around.

"Not a word of this to anyone, ya hear?" he said sternly with a frown on his face.

"Oh, of course. My lips are sealed, sir," I replied.

He nodded and walked off, lighting another fag. It wasn't my lips that I was worried about being opened. All the while home, I was sure that I was hearing someone following me. As I passed dark alleyways and opened abandoned homes, I saw all sorts of movement in the shadows, and when I called out, there were just whispers of wind.

I paid it no attention. There's nothing that I need to fear. I am a bobby of the Scotland Yard, and no one will be foolish enough to do anything to one of us. Plus, I never felt that we actually caught Jack the Ripper, but we were almost sure it was Thomas Wilschire. I always thought he was a wild one, just never the actual killer.

I chuckled as I left the tavern where I get my nightly dinner. As I walked into my two-bedroom home, there was a slight chill inside. I never feel the urge to have someone at my home as I do tonight. It is too cold and too dark and I am somehow afraid. I feel as though someone is here with me. My hair is standing up on the back of my neck as though caressed with a cold sliver of ice.

"Hello," I called out just now, feeling very foolish in doing so.

Of course, there was no answer. I did not focus on this; I just ate my beans and mash and lay across my bed. It is very difficult to sleep due to all the unanswered questions I have for Mr. Wilschire. Like, where did he go? All we saw was ashes in his room. And, what made him write down all the nasty deeds that he had committed? Was he as compelled as I was to do so? And, how did he escape with both doors locked and the windows sealed from the inside of the room? I do not understand any of this. I know I am not supposed to be thinking this deeply about this, or anything for that matter. I don't want to go back to my previous, darker days.

June 16, 1888

Jack the Ripper still on the loose!!
No new leads from Scotland Yard!!

"Oi, did you blab your mouth to anyone?" Blacksmith whispered to me, shoving the morning paper in my face. "In me office now!" he said sternly.

I shook my head in a "no" gesture and followed him as he turned inside.

"This bloke,--if it is Wilschire—is making us the laughing stock of Scotland Yard," he said, closing his office door.

I was quietly reading the paper and noticed how they had no names of who it possibly could be. Well, that was some sort of good news.

"Well, they don't know everything, sir. They have no names of anyone but the victims," I said.

"Well well, I'm gonna get ya a medal for 'at observation there, mate. We need results!! I refuse to look loike a fool; I could give two bullocks about the fokin names, 'Cliff!" he exclaimed.

His face was getting red and I could tell he was very upset about the whole situation. He stood in front of his large oak desk with his arms folded over his stomach. As I looked over his shoulder, I swear I could see a pair of eyes in the window above his shoulder. I squinted and rubbed my eyes. When I opened them, there was nothing there. Blacksmith snatched the paper from me.

"Get yaself some tea-- we need to go back to Wilschire's to see what else we can foind. I don't need ya at work all tired this week, for we got a lot to accomplish. Go and get together; you look like shite," he said, turning to sit behind his desk.

I went to the washing area and looked at myself in the mirror. I could tell instantly what Blacksmith was speaking about. I looked like shit. My face was extremely pale and my eyes were bloodshot as though I had been drinking all morning. What the hell was that that I had seen over his shoulder? I still cannot believe that I felt or saw a pair of eyes in the reflection behind him. They were not just staring, but glaring at me.

The more I think about it, I think there *are* actual whispers that I am hearing inside my head. I splashed cold water on my face and headed back out to the main investigation room. This is a very befuddling case to me indeed. Blacksmith isn't the only one this is taking a toll on. I look and feel as though I have aged about five years since I've taken up this whole case.

We went back to Wilschire's place to see what else we could find and where we went wrong. Going over his home with a fine tooth comb was very eerie, to be honest. We found many body parts tucked and hidden away, but the real distinct question about the whole kit and caboodle was, how in the hell did he leave his room? It made no sense. And as if he were reading my mind—

"How in the hell did he get outta here?" Blacksmith said aloud.

I haven't a clue, I said to myself.

But, I was very curious. Very curious indeed I was. What drove him to do such things?

"I'll be roight back; I need to speak with Vanschlatt. He may have an idea of something. I can't see this bloke going in and out and no one seeing him at all," Blacksmith said.

He left from Mr. Wilschire's bedroom.

"And let me know if ya foind somethin," he said, peeking back around the corner.

After he left, for some reason, I felt it become cool in the room. There was a moldy stench filling my nostrils and I began coughing with no control. My eyes began to water and I could barely stand. I then heard a woman's laughter from the bathing area. I couldn't help but move towards the laughing. As I rounded the corner, I could see a woman with yellow blond hair standing in the mirror. She was gorgeous. I could not help but stare at her. She looked in the mirror at me for a second and continued smiling. She was standing in the mirror, brushing her hair. Not only was it strange that she was in the lavatory, but also that she was comfortable with me seeing her completely naked.

"Excuse me madam, b-but there is an investigation going on right now and you can't be in the area disturbing the evidence," I said.

"Oh sorry, I did not know that was going on," she said without turning from the mirror.

Her eyes never left mine and I was at a loss for words. Her voice was beautiful and it sounded like a song. Her eyes shimmered like a running river. She was maddeningly beautiful.

"Well understood madam, but I will need to get your name because I need to know what your association with Mr. Wilschire is. I would also like to know how long you have been in here and—"

"Andrea," she cut me off.

"Pardon me?" I asked, licking my dry lips.

I noticed that my words caused vapor to form in front of my face. It was almost deathly cold now.

"My name is Andrea. And his name isn't Thomas either," she said, turning to show a perfect body.

I almost choked because her feet were not touching the ground, and I never said his first name.

"What in the bloody hell are ya doin,' Ratcliff?" I heard Blacksmith from behind me.

I jumped and spun around quickly. I didn't know what to say for a few seconds, and I just stared at him.

"I was talking to a wo--" I stopped myself to turn and point to Andrea.

I almost screeched like a bloody banshee! She was floating in front of the washbasin, jerking and shaking. Her skin was now a greyish purple with cracks; her eyes had rolled into the back of her head and then deflated. I know how it sounds as I write these words now, but her eyes deflated as though they were balloons and had lost all the air in them. Her face was dripping skin from it as though it were melting. She flew toward me and I fell back, but she then disappeared as I fell backward. Her laugh echoed in my head.

"Not now, Ratcliff. What the hell has gotten into ya?" he asked, almost screaming at me.

He reached down, picked me up off the ground, and all I could do was blabber a bunch of nothings. He began to shake me violently.

"I don't know what ya are trying to pull here, mate, but get yaself back on the roight bloody track roight bloody now or ya off tha case, mate!" now he was screaming at me. He actually slapped me.

That helped. I began to breathe normally and I lost the cobwebs that were on my mind. I was back to what could pass as normal.

"Sorry, sir. I think that my reflection may have scared me." I lied.

I couldn't tell him what I actually saw. Then I would really look bat shit crazy.

"I think I've been working too hard on this," I said.

"Well, let's get back to the station. Vanshlatt knew shit about his comings and goings. I need to read some more of that blasted diary," he said.

Blacksmith did not want to go to our chief inspector with the diary, but after reading the first few pages, I wanted to give the book to the inspector hastily. We sat back in his office, reading the diary. This was basically just his entire confession, and Blacksmith wasn't buying any of it.

"I haven't made up my mind completely yet, but tomorrow evening, I will know for sure what I want to do," he said after we finished reading the final page of Jack's, or actually Troy's, memoirs.

I watched him carefully place the booklet into his safety drawer and lock it as if it were to explode. For some reason, I had to hold back my laughter. He then sat at his chair with his fingers interlocked and under his nose with his elbows on his chair handles. I didn't know what was coming over me. But, from the back of my mind, I heard the same woman's voice from the bathroom, humming. I didn't understand this. I began to sweat somewhat and Blacksmith instantly picked up on it.

"Cliff, what's on you roight now? Ya look loike ya been runnin all day or something," he said.

"I'm fine," I snapped back to him.

I could tell he felt the shortness in my tone. I think the diary has had some sort of effect on us both. He was actually beginning to look rough himself.

"Question, 'ave you been getting enough sleep as of late? I mean I know we have been putting in a lot of hours with this whole case and all, but here lately, I've been not sleeping at all. What about you?" he asked, concerned.

"I can't really say. I think I have, but then again, I haven't," I responded.

He then reopened the drawer and handed me the diary.

"That settles it then. Take this bloody thing and burn it. I mean, burn it until there are nothing but ashes left. No one will even come close to believing this bullock about some ghostly wench making him kill all these people. I don't know why I even entertained this nonsense as long as I have. We will tell Inspector Lyons that we couldn't find anything tomorra. Got me?" he asked.

I felt the coolness of the book as it slid into my hands. For a moment, I actually thought it was breathing. I licked my lips as though I were going to actually kiss the damned thing. Andrea actually appeared behind him like a wispy cloud and smiled at me. For some reason, this made me want to laugh even more. Even with all these feelings, I wanted it out of my hands. I reached for a satchel that Blacksmith keeps on the top of his desk, emptied his items, and slid the book in their place.

"Oi mate, great idea. Burn that sack with it," he said, grabbing his fags, matches, notepad and uneaten lunch.

"I am right on it, sir," I said.

I could barely breathe. I felt massive pressure on me and I could not explain it. For some reason, I was worried. I felt as though someone would be there to assist me with this whole situation. I didn't know where this feeling of comfort came from, but I was aware it had something to do with the beauty I met in the bathroom. I left the yard and headed home.

I couldn't wrap my mind around why all this was happening to me. Why I was experiencing all this and Blacksmith wasn't. Well, he has not said anything about it. I could tell he wasn't experiencing what I was. He looked tired, but I looked as though I had been in a fight for sleep, so I was thinking that I needed to do what I was told to do with this journal.

I followed my usual routine of going to the pub and buying my ale and dinner for the evening. I arrived home to cold emptiness. Then, it hit me. I think I realized why I was experiencing all these crazy things. I don't have any outside family to distract me from it. I come home from work and this is all that I have to think about. But at this point, I welcome the thoughts. For some reason, listening to Andrea is like music to my mind. It seems to strengthen my soul. I sat at my table and realized that I am going insane. I grabbed the leather bound book, wrapped its string around the pages, picked up a lantern and took it to the back wooded area of my home.

Instead of the normal coolness that I had experienced previously, the journal now felt warm. In the steady darkness, it was cold and dark. There were no stars in the sky. I began to hear whispers in my head. This time it was not Andrea's voice I was hearing, but Mr. Wilschire's.

"*Burn it now,*" he urged me.

And, as if it were going to burst into flames at any moment, I felt the book in my hands begin to actually burn my fingers. I knew that I had to do this now or it would not happen. For some unexplainable reason, I was actually torn between doing the deed or not. If I didn't, what would I do? My answer hit me in the mind like a horse kick to the chest. A large gust of wind knocked me to the ground as though I were actually kicked. I clutched the smoking book to my chest, and for some reason I was unable to let it go.

"*Leave!!*" Andrea shouted at me.

The leaves rustled like cackling witches running across the cool grass. I had to complete this. I turned over, snatched one of my hands off the book, and gathered some of the leaves up into a tight pile. I ran into the house. By my back entrance, I found a piece of flint for starting fires and ran back outside. I tried and put the book on top of the leaves, but my hand was in a death clutch on the outer leather casing. This is when I became worried. My fingers finally began to feel the pain of the heat from inside the book itself. It had not completely reached through the leather cover until now. I dropped the flint that I had in my free hand and peeled my fingers open so the book was in my open palm.

"Let go!" I whispered into the darkness.

I was trying to ignore her rants and raves as she peeled back my mental defenses. This book of horrors would haunt this plane of existence no longer. Her form became more visible as I felt my sanity exiting my mind. I fell to my knees as I reached for more kindling as if I were building a twisted campfire for toasting marshmallows. The more she floated around me, the more I began to smell her putrid flesh burning my nose. I knew she was behind me, for I could feel her wintery breath making my neck hairs stand on end.

"We...nneeeed yooouu...to conti...uuuuu...," she seeped out with a raspy voice.

For some reason, I knew she was smiling without glancing over my shoulder. I could hear her jaws creaking like a door that hadn't been opened for years. I could feel the dry, brittle lips peeling back to reveal her grey, blackened teeth. I didn't dare look at her. I was afraid I would lose what grip I did have left on this world. The fear slipped away when I closed my eyes and I gained what little control I had in my hands.

They trembled as I reached for the tinder and flint rock. I squinted my eyes open just enough to see one of her grey skinned feet and snapped my eyes closed again. I remember, before closing them, seeing her toenails as grey as the sky before a heavy storm. They were hanging from her toes as if they were falling from her flesh. They seemed to be moving on their own from her toes, but as my mind readjusted, I knew they were bugs and maggots mixed in a dark fluid that I think was black, old blood turned into a thick, disgusting oil-like substance. My terrified fingers finally wrapped around the large flint stone and I struck the rock against the kindling twice. I then felt the first few droplets of rain fall on my head. Andrea cackled. The air was very cold out, but not as cold as her breath. Her hands clutched my shoulders and I felt the cold burn through my uniform. I knew then that there was no escape. Mr. Wilschire was no longer heard-- she had me. Andrea picked me up like a small child and turned me toward her while the rain pattered against my closed eyelids. She hummed a familiar tune from my childhood. This caused my eyes to open and I was blinded by daylight. I was in a large field of grass that extended for miles. Andrea was not holding my shoulders, but my mother.

"Daniel. It's time to wake up, Daniel. We have to go now," she hummed to me.

She reached up and moved a tendril of hair from my face.

"We have a boat to catch," she said to me softly as she took my hand.

"I know. We can't be late," I said with tears in my eyes.

My mother was very beautiful. Seeing her again after all these years brings emotions out of me that I cannot explain. Her skin was as smooth as buttermilk and her hair was a long, blonde blanket down her back. She smelled as though she bathed in fruits and roses.

"No, we can't be, for father is waiting. You know how upset he gets when we are not by his side," she urged in response.

She gently pulled me and we began our steps.

"Oh, Daniel, you are so absent-minded. Don't forget your toy your father just got you," she said.

I looked over my shoulder at the crisp, lush grass. I could hear cicadas in the distance making their normal, harmonizing noises. In the grass was a handmade constable carriage and horse laying on its side. I quickly scooped it in my free hand. It was ice cold to the touch, yet felt as though it belonged to me. My mother's hand was warm, and that was all that mattered. I don't know how long we walked, but it seemed forever in the bright sun. For some reason, my mother always wanted to go in between alleys and under walkways. As I walked behind her and she glanced at me in the shadows of the alley, her eyes seemed to have a distinct glow to them, like I was looking into an animal's eyes at a certain angle which would make them gleam their silvery glimmer. In my mind, I only heard her humming and this caused me no fear. We finally made it to our destination.

"All aboard to America!!!" I heard the fat, mustached man standing at the bottom of the boat ramp.

My mother was no longer at my side. I was no longer in my childish trance.

"Are you getting a ticket, sir?" the man asked.

"I don't have any--," I meant to say "coin" as I reached into my pocket with my free hand, but there was the exact cost in my pocket that I never put there.

I looked up the ramp to the entrance of the boat where people were flooding in to find a cabin to stay in, and there was my mother with her eyes giving me that silvery glimmer. I placed the payment in the man's hand, never taking my eyes of my mother. Clutching the book to my chest, I heard the boat master call for remaining people who wanted to get on. My mother disappeared around a corner. The humming was no longer in my ears. I could only hear the tide swashing against the metal of the boat.

I will continue what Thomas Wilschire could not. *I will see this to the end*, I thought to myself as I found an empty cabin to sit in. This will be a long trip but I will make it to this "Land of the Free." I chuckle, touching the leather that now feels like warm skin. I can tell Andrea is pleased with me. She floats down from the ceiling of the cabin and rests in my lap. I can only smile as she strokes my hair, and I have become accustomed to the smell of her rotting sorts. This book has helped me with that.

America.

www.ingramcontent.com/pod-product-compliance
Lightning Source LLC
Chambersburg PA
CBHW020645260626
47157CB00008B/2919